A GIRL HER HORSE AND A DOG

Terry Wolfe

For Emerson, Ruth and Hutch.

Love you all to the moon and back!

And to Misha and Sundance.

Faithful companions on four legs.

A big thanks to my editor Barry James Hickey who knows how to make a children's book come to life.

And to my illustrator Benjamin Hummel for allowing us to see them.

A Girl, Her Horse, and a Dog

ISBN-13: 978-1517173593

ISBN-10: 1517173590

CHAPTER 1

THE 4-H CLUB

The young members of the 4-H Club met every Thursday after school at the community center.

Josephine Wilson sat in the back of the meeting hall, her baseball cap pulled low on her forehead. She was a tadpole of a kid, still waiting for her legs and arms to catch up to her nine-year old imagination.

"Jo's as scrawny as a scarecrow," her mischievous cousin Todd liked to say. He lived next to Jo's ranch with his younger sister Hannah.

The 4-H team leader was calling on the other kids, one by one, asking them what their annual projects would be.

Billy Fanaway wanted to raise a billy goat. Becky Dolan was going to hatch baby ducks from eggs. Kevin Hogan and his mean sister Tami were going to teach and train a companion dog for the blind.

Josephine's cousin Hannah told the group one of her horses named April was going to have a new colt or filly. "And I'm going to raise her."

"You'll have your hands full for sure," smiled the 4-H leader. "What about you, Todd?" the leader asked.

"I started chickens last year. Already got a turkey for this year."

Luke Ford jumped up from his seat and took off his cowboy hat. "Me and Todd are also going to learn team-roping. We'll be the best cowpokes in the county!" Luke glanced at Jo and winked. "You can bet your bottom dollar on it."

Jo shrank in her seat. She always shrank when Luke Ford gave her notice. He looked clean-cut with pressed jeans, a yoked shirt and a flat top haircut. He was Todd's best friend.

One by one, kids stood up and shared their plans.

"And finally Josephine Wilson," the team leader said. "What is your project, Jo?"

Jo squirmed out of her seat and stood up, uncomfortable that everyone had turned to stare at her. She wasn't invisible now. She had been thinking for weeks about her project and had finally come to a decision.

"I'm getting a dog," she said.

"Oh?" said the instructor. "A pet?"

"No. A working dog for my family ranch. We have a hundred head of cattle and not enough hands."

"A herding dog?" said the team leader.

"Yes. The best one in the whole county," Jo added.

Todd laughed in his seat. "This I gotta see."

"Mind your own business," said Jo.

"We live next door to you," Todd pressed. "If that dog isn't trained proper, it'll be a stray, comin' over to our place all the time, lookin' for food. Maybe kill all my chickens."

"I can do this," Jo told the instructor. "My dog won't be any ordinary sit-on-the-porch-and-bark-at-squirrels dog but a herding, circling, nose-to-the-ground *cow dog*."

Luke Ford stood up and removed his cowboy hat. "If Jo Wilson says she can do it, I believe her." He turned to her, did his wink and sat back down.

Jo shrank back in her chair but smiled this time. She didn't understand why Luke Ford paid any attention to her but she sort of liked that he did sometimes.

The 4-H leader wrote down Jo's project on a clipboard. "It's settled then. Everyone has an assigned task for the year of 1956. Good luck to you all."

Todd wasn't done with his pestering. "By the time my cousin Jo Wilson is done with that dog, it'll only have one eye and three legs," he laughed.

His younger sister Hannah poked him hard in the side. "Stop being mean," she said.

Jo pulled her hat as low as she could to hide the emerging tears in her eyes. She crossed her arms, glaring at her bigger cousin. "I'll show you, Todd Marshall. Just you wait and see."

CHAPTER 2

A DOG FOR SALE

The next morning Jo ran to the yellow box out by the road and retrieved the morning newspaper. At the kitchen table she carefully dismantled the newspaper by sections. Besides running a ranch with a hundred head of cattle, her father Charlie was a doctor in Colorado Springs. He always started his day scanning the paper's national and local news.

"Looking for the comics, Jo?" her dad asked as he poured himself a cup of coffee from the aluminum pot on the stove.

"I need a dog," Jo said.

"A dog!" her father said. "This have to do with 4-H?"

"Yes." Jo held the classifieds in her hand and gave the rest of the paper to her dad.

Anne Wilson came in next, wearing work gloves and carrying a pail of fresh milk.

"Jo needs a dog," Mr. Wilson told his wife.

"It's about time!" declared Anne.

"Then it's okay?" said Jo.

"Sure," said her parents.

"But not just any dog. A cattle dog," said Jo. She scanned the pages of the newspaper, her eyes narrowed. "Where do I look?"

"Try 'Puppies for Sale,'" said her mom.

"Owning a dog is a big responsibility," said her dad. "Just like the horses."

"I know," said Jo, her nose buried behind the paper. "What kind of dog should we get?"

"Well," Charlie said, scratching his morning stubble. "Certain dogs do certain things. You don't want a Chihuahua. Stay clear of poodles and basset hounds. Some mutts are good..."

Jo's parents pulled up chairs on either side and scanned the classifieds with her.

"For my money the best dogs for cattle are blue heelers and border collies," said Charlie.

"Is that true?" Jo asked her mother.

"They're built right. Thick legs and stamina," said her mom.

"And they're smart," said Charlie.

"Here's one for German shepherd pups," said Jo.

"They don't herd well," said her dad. "Too much strain on their hips."

"What about this one? Laboratory... Labrador retriever?"

"Best used for hunting," said Charlie Wilson. His finger pointed at the paper. "Now this is interesting," he read aloud: "Moving to the city. Free border collie for the right owner. Seven year old female. Great temperament. Loves the ranch life. Has her shots. Neutered."

"What does it mean 'neutered'?" Jo asked.

"She can't have pups," said her father.

Jo set the paper down. "I don't know... this dog's near old as me."

"And she needs a good home," said Mrs. Wilson.

"A dog like this will be hard to place," said Mr. Wilson.

"What if nobody takes her?" Jo said.

Charlie sipped his coffee. "She could end up at the animal shelter. If nobody picks her there, they'll put her to sleep."

"That's terrible!" said Jo. She picked up the newspaper again. "Loves the ranch life," she read aloud.

Her parents didn't say anything, just sat there calm as can be.

"I'd like to take a look at this dog if it's okay by you," Jo told her parents. "Her name is *Misha*."

"Pretty name," said her mother.

"For all we know, Misha may already have some training," said Charlie. "With a well-trained dog you can go everywhere. Your mom and I both had dogs when we were young."

"But they are a responsibility," reminded Mrs. Wilson. "Dogs need constant attention."

"And affection," added Jo's dad.

Jo smiled at her parents. "You are so wise."

"I hope you say that when you are a teenager," her dad said with a laugh. He took the paper from Jo. "I'll call today when I get to my office. We just finished calving season. It would be good to have an experienced dog around the newborns. Maybe we can see her when you're done with school."

"Oh my gosh! It's the last day of school!" Jo realized. She stared at the wall clock. She only had ten minutes to catch the bus.

CHAPTER 3

GETTING MISHA

Jo was anxious to get home. She had said her goodbyes to most of the kids for the summer on the steps of the school. It had rained all morning and half of the afternoon. The tires of the school bus made great splashes in the puddles of water that had formed in the potholes as it wound its way on the country road taking the students home from school.

It was springtime in the foothills below Pikes Peak. The aspen trees were clad in their full attire of bright green leaves of various shades and shapes, all singing to each other as they rustled in the breeze like an orchestra of flutes. The Douglas fir and lodge pole pines of various heights appeared to be fastened together on the hills and mountain sides. Scrub oaks were ready to break out their buds into odd-shaped leaves at any moment. The expanses of native grama grass turning green in the pastures were decorated with Blue-Eyed grass, Fireweed, and Crimson Saxifrage. The bloom of wildflowers was a riot of color in contrast to the yellow bus.

In the middle of this striking and colorful landscape sat two ranches divided by a fence lined with aspen trees.

One ranch, a white house with a red trim and a matching barn with a large haystack to its right was owned by the Marshalls. The other ranch owned by the Wilsons had a pale yellow house with a wraparound porch and white trim and a red barn with two large black doors.

The two ranches were once one. Originally owned by Henry and Elizabeth Penner, Jo's grandparents, they had lived in the red trimmed house, raising registered Quarter Horses and Hereford cattle for show and sale.

They had two daughters; Jo's mother Anne and her aunt Claire.

Grandpa Henry once said to his daughters, "This place is in your blood and you must return."

Over the years their daughters, "after seeing the world" as Grandpa Henry called it, did return home to continue the ranching business with their husbands, Charles Wilson and John Marshall. Besides ranching, Charlie was a family doctor. John Marshall owned and ran a popular feed store.

Over the years the houses remained the haven of love, laughter, and close relationships that kept the extended family strong.

A hundred Hereford cattle and their young calves grazed on the flowers in the Wilson pasture. On the other side of a wire fence line than ran along a narrow creek, the Marshall's herd of ninety-five cows and their calves did the same. The creek only held water in the late spring and summer after a good rain.

Jo eyed her cousin Todd. He was two years older than her and not as tall as his younger sister Hannah.

Todd was handsome, even for a boy. His dark hair seemed almost black in the sun and his piercing brown eyes mimicked his self-assured smile and easy countenance. His teachers always took his side regardless if his homework was late. He was that kind of boy.

Todd was a good older brother to Hannah, protective but always eager to tease. With Jo living next door, he had two easy targets with plenty of opportunities.

He never sat with Jo and Hannah on the bus. Boys sat with boys, girls sat with girls. Boys had their secrets, girls had theirs. Jo didn't care for the whispers and gossip of the bus. Whenever she looked at Todd who always sat in the back, Todd seemed to always be plotting out some secret with his best friend Luke. If

Jo looked back too long, Luke always caught her staring at him and winked back at her.

Hannah was tall and slim for a ten year old. She had soft brown eyes. "Doe eyes," said her mother. She wore her long brown hair pulled back into a ponytail topped by a ball cap most of the time. For Hannah and Jo dresses were only for church.

At nine years old, Jo was the youngest of the three. She too had brown hair, a little darker than Hannah's, and spunky dark brown eyes. She wore her hair like Hannah in a ponytail with a ball cap on top. Some of the school kids said they acted and looked like sisters.

Besides being cousins, Jo and Hannah were best friends and kindred spirits. Only a month ago they vowed an oath of deep enduring friendship until death while riding their horses, holding each other's reins in their left hand and grasping right hands so their arms crossed on top of each other. They promised that their friendship would last to the moon and back, and then some.

It was a giant promise to keep.

Sally Stroud, the school's chatterbox destined for a career in theater usually sat across from Hannah and Jo on the bus, sharing the latest news in fashion, movies and music. Her favorite film of all time was *TAMMY* starring Debbie Reynolds. Sally was an indifferent student in the classroom but Sally got straight A's when it came to the entertainment world far away from their country lives. Sally's parents took her to musical plays at least twice a year and once a month Sally got to go to the new drive-in theater in town to see the double-features.

When the school bus came to a stop in front of the Marshall ranch, Hannah waved goodbye to Jo before she and Todd jumped off the bus together and raced down the long drive towards their house.

"Good luck getting a dog today!" Hannah shouted.

"Make sure you check for ticks and lice," said Todd.

Jo got off the bus a half mile down the road and raced up the long drive to the barn and found her father outside cleaning Bells' and Checkers' corral. They were known as *the co-eds* among family and friends. Bell was a buckskin Appaloosa mare born on December 22nd. Her registered name was Silver Bells. She was one of the top reining horses in the country. Checkers was a dark bay color and a great cow pony. Jo's dad also used him for roping.

"How was school today?" her father asked.

"Okay. How was work?"

"Okay. Mrs. Miller's arthritis flared up again. Old Elijah Brewster still insists he doesn't need reading glasses. Perry Masterson fell in his bathtub again."

"Do you like being a doctor?" Jo said.

"I like helping people," said Charlie Wilson. "And it helps pay for the ranch."

"Did you ever want to just be a full-time cowboy?"

"No," decided her dad. "This ranch is big enough. We can manage our small herd of livestock year in and out."

Jo's dad continued raking the manure as Jo opened the gate and walked in. Both horses walked over to her. She set her school bag down and rubbed their noses.

"Did Bell and Checkers get their daily exercise?" she asked her father.

"Yep. Still need to be fed. Don't forget Sundance."

"Did you check on that dog?"

"Yep. She's still available," he said as he raked.

"Are we going to see her like you promised?"

"Just as soon as you finish your chores. Remember what your mom and I said about responsibility?"

"Sure. I remember."

He handed her the rake and smiled. "Don't forget to run Sundance, too. He needs his daily exercise. I already saddled him for you. While you ride, I'll run feed out for the cattle."

Her dad picked up her school bag and carried it towards the house.

Jo finished filling a wheelbarrow with dirty hay, fed Bell and Checkers and led Sundance out of the barn. Sundance was a red roan Appaloosa with striped hooves and big eyes that gave him an expressive humanlike gaze.

She climbed a fence post and threw her legs over him.

"Let's go, Sundance," Jo commanded. "Duck pond."

The horse trotted behind the barn with her, heading towards the pond at the back of one of the pastures. There were five ducks on the water, bobbing their heads beneath the surface for minnows and insects. Jo just knew Sundance loved watching them as much as she did. She wondered if the same ducks went from pond to pond at all the other local ranches.

"Just think, Sundance! Maybe this new dog will like to swim in this old muddy cow pond and chase ducks with us," she said laughing out loud.

Jo laid the reins on Sundance's neck and gave him a gentle nudge with her heels to his sides. They rode off toward the tall pine trees on the hill. After a good gallop through the thin pine forest along the old Jeep Road, Jo turned Sundance towards the ranch.

"Thanks for listening, Sundance. I think you will agree that a new dog as a companion will be good."

Her father was waiting for her at the barn. He helped Jo remove Sundance's saddle and rig and handed her a brush.

"Almost done," he said.

"What about my dog?" she said as she let out a long breath.

"Patience, daughter. One thing at a time." After Mr. Wilson carried the tack into the barn, he headed for the house.

Jo fed Sundance and gave him a good brushing. Jo's eyes glanced towards the house every thirty seconds until she saw her parents emerge.

"Put Sundance in the corral with Bell and Checkers," her dad yelled with a smile. "And don't take all day. We have to see a man about a dog!"

Jo's mom was smiling too.

"Should we take the station wagon or the truck?" asked Mr. Wilson.

"Whichever is closer!" said Jo.

In less than a minute, Jo was sitting in the truck between her parents. Her mom handed her a map.

"Think you can read this?" she said.

"I'll try," said Jo. "What did the man say about Misha?"

"His name is Hank Wills. He said the dog is still available," said her father.

"Misha means 'bear' in Russian," Mrs. Wilson said as a matter of fact.

"How do you know that?" Jo asked

"Moms know all kinds of things," Anne Wilson said.

"I know something, too," said Jo. "One of my teachers told me that many people consider border collies the world's best herding dog. Bar none. They're quick, too. They don't drive the herd away from the handler like most herding dogs. They circle the cows and bring them back to the handler. Border collies move along with a crouch and they use eye contact to stare the animals down and move them in the right direction."

"Intimidation as a tool," said her dad.

"And if the dog's stare doesn't work, then they bark, nip, and bite at the heels until the livestock moves. Maybe I'll get lucky. Maybe Misha is already a herding dog."

"Wouldn't that be something," said Charlie Wilson.

They drove twenty miles east out towards the plains that tapered off from the eastern range of the mountains. Jo realized she didn't have the particulars required to read a road map and handed it to her mom.

"Go another mile then turn right," her mother instructed her father. "Then turn on County Road 20."

As Charlie Wilson drove, Anne Wilson gave Jo some advice. "It will take time, patience, and consistency to work with Misha even though she is older and knows something."

"You and dad had dogs once. Will you help me?"

"Of course we will," said her parents.

Mrs. Wilson gave new directions onto Wiggins Road until they found the Wills ranch with a red barn and a big hay stack next to it.

Charlie pulled the truck up next to the barn. There was a large apple tree in the middle of the yard. Blue iris and white daisies had scattered themselves around the white fences and gates. When the three got out of the truck, an elderly man came out of the house waving.

"You must be the Wilson gang. I bet you came to see Misha," he said with a smile. "I'm Hank Wills. Misha is on the back porch. Follow me."

The Wilsons followed Hank Wills around to the back of the house.

There sat Misha looking proud as can be. Her red sable coat was clean and shiny. She cocked her head with her ears up, looking right at Jo.

Jo's eyes lit up. "She's beautiful!"

Misha stood up and started wagging her tail. Jo ran to her and knelt down. She patted Misha on the head and rubbed her back.

"Well," said Hank Wills. "I think Misha likes you! Like I told you over the phone, Mr. Wilson, she's cow and horse savvy. I haven't taught her any formal herding skills but she's a quick study. She'll give you her all, pound for pound."

"Hello sweet thing," said Jo, hugging her.

Misha licked Jo's cheek.

"I'd say we got a match," said Mrs. Wilson.

"Hate to lose her, but I'm selling the place," said Mr. Wills. "My wife had a stroke a few months ago. She's doing better, but we can't take any chances with her health being way out here in the country. I can't see Misha boxed up. Wouldn't be fair to her."

"Can I take her for a walk?" Jo said.

"Sure," said Mr. Wills. "Hope you can keep up."

Jo and Misha ran together towards an open field, dancing and tripping over each other like long lost friends.

"Now that's what I call a match," said Mr. Wills.

"Jo will take good care of her," promised Anne Wilson.

Mr. Wills sighed. "Hate to see Misha go, but she looks to be in good hands."

After a long hike and over a cold pitcher of fresh lemonade, Jo and Misha sat together on the porch steps listening to the adults sharing their own dog stories from their childhoods.

"There's nothing like a good dog," Mr. Wills said. "Better than some people." He looked down at Jo. "She's yours, young lady. All fifty pounds of her."

"Thank you, Mr. Wills."

"I may be old, but I ain't dead," he added. "If you folks need help in her training, I'd be glad to participate. You know my telephone number. I'm available most any time."

Jo thanked Hank Wills over and over again. Then she said, "Come on, Misha lets go home."

Misha followed her and jumped in the truck as if she had done it a hundred times before.

Driving away from the Wills ranch, Jo waved her arm out the window to Mr. Wills and he waved back. She turned and hugged Misha.

"What do you think?" Charlie asked his wife.

"I think Jo has a new best friend," said Anne.

"I can't wait to show Hannah!" said Jo.

"What about Todd?" asked her mom.

"Todd can see Misha after *he* takes a bath," said Jo. "I don't want her catching his fleas."

Everyone laughed as they headed west towards the mountains, their faces awash in the glow of a red sunset.

"This is the best day of my life so far," Jo decided. "Better than Christmas!"

CHAPTER 4

MISHA'S NEW HOME

Claire Marshall stood in the doorway of the Wilson kitchen with her sister Anne watching Jo and Hannah playing with Misha on the floor.

"She's beautiful, Jo!" said Hannah.

"And smart too!" Jo bragged. "Can Hannah stay for dinner?" she asked her mother.

"That will be fine," said Anne. She looked at Claire. "I'll run her home afterwards."

"Don't be a pest," Claire told her daughter. "And help with the dishes when you're done."

"I will," promised Hannah, her hands petting Misha in all directions.

Misha crawled over the girls and sniffed at Hannah's jacket.

"What's she doing?" asked Hannah.

"Smelling your horses, I'll bet," said Claire Marshall.

"Okay girls," ordered Mrs. Wilson. "Play with Misha outside for half an hour while I cook dinner, then fetch your dad in the barn."

Jo and Hannah raced outside, tripping over anxious Misha as she ran between their legs.

Anne and Claire smiled at the sight.

"I think she's got one heck of a dog," said Claire.

"I hope so," said Anne. "Misha definitely has spunk."

"Seems smart, too."

"Let's hope she isn't too smart."

After dinner Hannah helped Jo wash and dry the dishes as promised.

"How come your parents named you Josephine?" Hannah asked as she dried a plate.

"My mom says when she was a little girl she read a book called *Little Women*. Her favorite character was a girl named Josephine. Jo for short. She told my dad if she ever had a girl she wanted to name me Josephine."

"Do you want me to call you Josephine from now on?"

"I like Jo better."

"Okay, Jo. I'll save Josephine for special occasions."

"How did you get the name Hannah?"

"It's biblical."

"Oh."

"Say," said Hannah. "Have you listened to the radio lately?"

"No. Why?"

"I heard this new singer named Elvis Presley."

"Is he any good?"

"I didn't get to hear the whole song. My mom changed the channel to Tommy Dorsey. She said his orchestra was easier on her ears than a screaming wildcat."

When the girls finished the dishes Charlie Wilson volunteered to drive Hannah home. Jo and Misha joined them in the truck.

"Todd can't wait to see your new dog," said Hannah.

"Really?" said Jo.

"How's he doing with his turkey?" asked Mr. Wilson.

"Todd says he doesn't like him much," said Hannah. "The chickens don't like him either."

"What's he going to do?"

"Todd is trying to sell him. He says he doesn't want the chores but I don't believe him."

"Why not?"

"He treats his turkey like a pet. Calls him Tom. And we know what's supposed to happen to that dumb bird come Thanksgiving."

Hannah dragged her finger across her neck. Jo smiled to herself.

"What's so funny?" said Hannah.

"I didn't think Todd was that sensitive," said Jo. "How is his roping coming along?"

"He's getting the hang of it. Todd and Luke Ford have been practicing twice a week with the hay bales. My dad rigged up some horns to it. They can't last an hour without getting bored before they hop the fence and go runnin' off with their BB guns."

Mr. Wilson steered the truck onto the road and drove the half mile between the Wilson house and the entrance to the Marshall ranch. He turned up the long gravel drive to the Marshall's big white house.

Todd was sitting on the front porch, elbows on his knees and his chin in his hands.

"Why does Todd look so sad?" Jo said.

"Maybe because you didn't invite him to see Misha earlier," said her father.

"I suppose I better fix things," Jo decided.

When the truck came to a stop Jo swung open the door and led Misha to Todd. Misha bounded up the steps and licked His face.

Todd rubbed Misha behind the ears and playfully wrestled with her. "What's her name?"

"Misha," said Jo.

"Looks to be a good cow dog," Todd said.

"Really?" said Jo.

"Oh, yeah," said Todd, petting Misha all over. "Good eyes, good coat of fur, strong bones. You got lucky with this one."

"She's already an adult but she'll still need some training."

"I can help you!" Todd said.

"What about your tom turkey?"

"Oh, that danged crazy bird. I can't teach him nuthin'. Wish I got me a dog instead."

"We can share her sometimes," said Jo.

"Really?" said Todd.

"Sure. Why not?"

She had never seen Todd with such a big and genuine smile before.

"Dogs like me," he said. "Misha and I will get along great. You'll see."

Mr. and Mrs. Marshall came out of the house and fawned over Misha. Everyone agreed she was a fine dog.

CHAPTER 5

RIDE TO PIKEVIEW

A few days passed. The first tradition of summer was about to be kept when Jo called Hannah at her house.

"It's time to celebrate no school and a big yeah for the beginning of summer. Let's ride April and Sundance to Pikeview for our first ice cream of the summer."

"Okay," Said Hannah. "I'll meet you in thirty minutes at the gate."

Jo went to the barn, gave Sundance a quick brush, checked his hooves and gave him an apple to distract him while she saddled him for the ride. Next she dropped the halter and slipped on his headstall and led him out of the barn. She climbed a fence rail and jumped on his back.

She saw her mom and yelled out to her. "Mom I 'm meeting Hannah and we are riding for ice cream. Please call Mrs. Reed at the country store and let her know we are coming!"

"See you in a while," said her mom. "Are you taking Misha?"

"Yes."

"Have Mrs. Reed call me before you head back so we don't worry," said her mom.

"Okay."

Jo pulled her ball cap down to make sure it was secure and to keep the sun from her eyes. "Let's go, Misha."

Misha rose from the shade of a tree and trotted behind Jo and Sundance, wagging her tail.

Jo arrived a little before Hannah at the gate. She got off Sundance and lay down in the new grass that was starting to come up. Sundance started to graze and Misha stretched out in the sun next to Jo. The three were each in their own world.

"What are you doing?" Asked Hannah as she rode up on April and saw the three.

"I am just thinking how happy I am that all of summer is before us, how good our first ice cream cone is going to taste, and how I will miss the sound of the morning dove while we wait for the school bus," said Jo.

"Well, get up and get on Sundance and let's go!" Hannah said. "I will miss the sound of the birds but not getting up early and going to school." She nudged April with a tap of her heels.

Jo got up and climbed in her saddle.

"Pretty good!" Hannah said. "Looks like you don't need a fence post anymore!"

Sundance started trotting after April and Hannah.

"Come on. Misha," called Jo.

Misha stood and caught up.

The large pasture they rode through was green with lush grama grass and wildflowers of Indian paint brush, bluebells, and blue-eyed grass showing their brilliant colors mixed with the bright green of new grass.

There was a large pond and windmill in the pasture. For years the Wilsons and Marshalls shared the pasture in the summer for the cattle. The grass was thick and tall and water was plentiful in the pond.

At times mallard ducks would fly over and stop to swim and rest at the pond. Geese would also use this pond on their migration trips in the fall and early spring.

"Hannah, we need to stop at the pond to see if any ducks have landed. You know how Sundance likes to watch the ducks," Jo said.

"Oh you are such a dreamer and your imagination is so amazing. Only you would think that Sundance, who is a horse I might add, likes to watch ducks swim."

"Well, he does. Really! I know my horse. He even gives a sigh of 'all is well' when he sees them."

"You are shocking with that imagination of yours," said Hannah. She turned April towards the pond, following Jo and Sundance.

Sundance reached the water's edge. Jo bent over in the saddle and put her face on his neck and talked to him. "There are your ducks, Sundance. See them swimming?" She looked at Hannah. "I told you he likes to watch them."

Hannah rolled her eyes and turned April towards a trail. "Jo, you are such a dreamer! Can we please get our ice cream now?"

Jo let out a soft sigh. "Come on, Sundance. Let's go."

As Pikeview come into view down in the eastern foothills, Hannah asked Jo, "What kind of ice cream are you going to get this year? Oh, let me guess. Vanilla! Right?"

"Yep," said Jo.

"Do you ever eat any other flavor?"

"No. Just vanilla."

"I don't understand how a girl with such an active imagination can only get boring vanilla," said Hannah.

"It's not boring. It's like a blank piece of paper or canvas. I imagine anything I want with it when I eat it. How about you?"

"I can't ever decide," sighed Hannah. "I keep thinking between vanilla, chocolate, or strawberry. It is such a hard choice. Do you suppose I could have a little of each to make one scoop?"

This time Jo rolled her eyes and shook her head.

The sun was warm with no clouds in the sky. The girls sat on their horses at the top of a hill for a minute, studying the land below.

Pikeview was a small coal mining town. There was a cluster of small houses with white siding that had turned pale gray from coal dust. There was a train track running parallel to the town. The coal train came through once a week to fill cars with coal heaped liked small mountains in each car.

An old cottage that was now a general store sat in the center. There were metal signs advertising Purina Dog Chow and Coca Cola attached to the walls. The store carried small quantities to supply the basic needs of the community. It also sold ice cream.

The girls led their horses down a slope to the single street of the small town towards the general store. They threw the reins over a hitching post rail and tied their horses to it. Jo jumped on the porch with Hannah right behind and opened the screen door.

Mrs. Reed, the store owner was standing behind a small counter, wearing the same loose gingham dress she had been wearing the previous summer.

"Well, if it isn't Miss Josephine and Miss Hannah!" smiled Mrs. Reed. "My, how you girls have grown!"

"Hi, Mrs. Reed," said Jo.

"Hello again," said Hannah behind her in the doorway.

"Your mom called, Jo. She said you can eat as much ice cream as you can hold."

"On credit?" said Jo.

"We'll settle up at the end of summer. Just like always."

Misha squeezed past the girls and trotted up to Mrs. Reed.

"What have we here?" said Mrs. Reed.

"Got me a dog," said Jo proudly. "Her name is Misha. Are dogs allowed inside?"

"Only on their first visit," smiled Mrs. Reed. She came from behind the counter and patted Misha on the head. "A fine dog, Jo. Really fine! Hello, Misha! Let me get you a bowl of water."

She pulled an old chipped pottery bowl from under the counter, filled it with water and set it on the floor for Misha. Misha happily lapped at the cool water, gratitude in her eyes.

Hannah jumped on a red vinyl stool, her chin in her hands, looking up at the short list of ice creams posted on the wall behind the long marble counter. She read her choices out loud.

"Chocolate, vanilla, strawberry, chocolate, vanilla, strawberry... I just can't make up my mind!"

Jo smiled and sat next to her. "Don't tell me you still can't decide. There are only three choices."

"How about you, Jo?" said Mrs. Reed. "The usual?"

"Yes. Vanilla, please."

"And for you, Hannah?" Mrs. Reed asked with a smile.

"Oh!" said Hannah, shaking her head. "Get Jo's vanilla! I am still thinking."

Mrs. Reed grabbed a scooper, opened the ice cream case and dug into a large container of freshly churned ice cream. She placed a large scoop of vanilla in an ice cream cone and handed it across the counter to Jo.

"Thank you," Jo said reaching for the cone.

"You are welcome. Hannah? Are you ready? Ice cream's melting."

Hannah let out a long sigh with her decision. "I will start the summer off with strawberry," she said.

"Strawberry it is," said Mrs. Reed as she reached for an ice cream cone.

Misha stood up and nudged her nose against Jo's leg.

"Looks like your dog wants a cone too," laughed Mrs. Reed.

"If she's like Jo, she probably wants vanilla," said Hannah.

The girls carried their cones outside and sat on the porch, hanging their legs off the edge as they licked at the sides of their dripping ice cream.

Jo pushed her ball cap back. "Isn't this just grand?"

Misha sat next to her, looking to Jo to give her a lick or a bite. Her tail wagged and thumped on the porch. There was an impossible dog smile on her face. Jo took one last bite and gave Misha the last piece of cone with a hint of ice cream on it.

Jo stood up and looked at Hannah. Hannah popped the bottom of her cone in her mouth and savored the flavor.

"Are you ready to ride?" asked Jo.

"I am."

Mrs. Reed came outside and watched the young girls as they saddled up.

"Don't grow up too quick now," she said. "Enjoy your summer. Every day of it."

"See you next week," said Hannah.

"I'll be here," said Mrs. Reed.

The girls checked their saddle cinches, put the reins over their horses' heads and got on.

"Let's go home," Jo said to Misha on the porch.

Misha leapt off the porch facing the street they rode in on.

"Look at Misha!" said Mrs. Reed. "Only her first trip here and she knows her way back. That's a mighty fine dog you got there, Jo."

"Thanks," Jo said.

"I'll call your mom and let her know you're headed home."

The girls waved as they started home with Misha in the lead.

CHAPTER 6

THE SHORT SUMMER

The warming days of summer went by too quickly. Jo helped her mom prepare jams and jellies from the local fruit trees. She watered the flower beds and pulled weeds with her bare hands. Jo loved the feel and smell of the dirt between her fingers. Misha liked the feel of dirt too. Jo carried a small rag in her back pocket to wipe Misha's paws and nose clean whenever they went in the house.

Jo also helped her dad with some of the daily chores that ranch life required; cleaning pens and stalls, feeding the animals and keeping them safe.

She loved leading Misha out to the pastures and watched as Misha instinctively moved between the cows and calves. If Misha heard a calf crying she would run up to it, sniff it, search among the herd, find its mother and drive her back to the baby. Jo was dumbfounded by this. To her most of the cattle looked alike. How Misha knew who belonged to who amazed her.

The high chaparral of the foothills provided scant grass due to the limited rainfall. It took more acres of wild grass to feed a cow than the lush plains of the Midwest. This made for a herd of scattered animals.

When feeding time came around Misha would go to the farthest part of the pasture where a cow stood, lower her head and force the cow to move ahead with the rest of the herd. She ran fast in big looping circles or zig-zagged back and forth, never letting the cows turn back as she nipped at their legs. Though the cows were twenty times her size, Misha seemed to be in charge. Jo learned that the cows, dumb as they were, responded easily to daily routines that involved a reward of water, wild grass or the feed lot.

Misha could sit for hours on end in the pasture, watching the cattle as they patiently grazed. She was a cow dog alright!

On the Fourth of July, the Wilsons and Marshalls drove into town for a backyard barbecue at Grandpa and Grandma Penner's house.

Now retired, Grandpa Henry loved grilling hamburgers, hot dogs and steaks as he listened to his sons-in-law Charlie Wilson and John Marshall talk about the goings-on of their respective ranches.

"I always told my daughters you can't go wrong with cattle," Grandpa Henry liked to say. "America loves a good steak."

Grandma Elizabeth kept her daughters busy in the kitchen preparing dishes of fruits and salads and fresh vegetables. Anne and Claire seemed more like girls than mothers around her. She still wasn't done raising them in some ways.

Jo, Hannah and Todd had their share of chores, too; shucking corn, setting the picnic table and clearing the dishes.

Misha spent her day digging for worms in the dirt along the fence or barking at the pesky squirrels in the trees teasing her with their chatter.

When it grew dark, everyone walked to the local city park for the annual fireworks display put on by the city.

Jo held Misha on her lap as they watched the sky fill with bursting colors of red, blue, yellow and silver. It was a wonderful day. On the drive back home Jo fell asleep in the backseat of the station wagon with Misha's head tucked in her lap.

Jo rode Sundance almost every day, sometimes accompanied by Hannah. At least once a week Todd joined the girls for a ride.

Jo never went anywhere without Misha at her side. Misha had taken to the ranch quickly. Misha was fond of Mr. and Mrs. Wilson and the Marshall family, but it was clear to everyone that she was Jo's dog. Misha adored Jo and Jo loved her back with equal enthusiasm.

Sometimes Jo and Misha would walk over to the Marshall ranch to watch Todd and his friend Luke practice their roping skills. As summer progressed, the boys went from standing on their feet tossing ropes at hay bales to riding on horseback and snagging calves in the corral.

Once in a while Luke would walk over to Jo at the fence and ask how she was doing.

"Alright, I guess," Jo always said.

Luke made her feel funny inside.

Inch by inch, the kids grew and the calves added pounds.

The long days of summer slowly dwindled to an end.

CHAPTER 7

A NEW FILLY

The first day of school was coming all too soon.

Anne Wilson insisted Jo take a one-hour bath to wipe away the grit and grime of summer for a "fresh start."

Misha got a bath next. She didn't fight when Jo's dad lifted her into the bathtub but when Jo poured that first cup of warm water over Misha's head, Misha looked at her like a dog betrayed.

"You're a girl," Jo insisted. "Sometimes you have to look pretty and smell nice."

After the Wilsons toweled off Misha she ran outside and rolled in the grass for half an hour.

"So much for smelling pretty," Jo fumed.

The day before school was to start Jo and Hannah rode their horses to Pikeview for the last ice cream of summer. Hannah had chocolate. Jo had vanilla. The girls paid Mrs. Reed their tab in full and promised to see her next summer.

The first day of school went by quickly with all the kids catching up on their summer adventures.

"But mine's not quite over yet!" Hannah bragged to her schoolmates. "Any day now, my mare April is going to drop her foal."

"I may have to skip a few days of school to help her," Todd told one of his teachers.

Every day after school on the bus ride home, Hannah fidgeted in her seat, anxious to check on things at home.

"Today could be the day," she told Jo.

December was several months away, but Sally Stroud, a girl born to be an actress, was already preparing for her annual performance in the Christmas Pageant. "Perhaps we could put your new filly in the manger with the other animals."

When the bus stopped on the road by the Marshall mailbox Hannah and Todd ran all the way to the barn, out of breath.

John Marshall put out his big suntanned arm to slow them down. "Easy now, pull up the reins!" he said.

"Did April have her baby today?" Hannah asked.

"Yes she did," John Marshall said with a smile.

"What did she have?" said Todd, catching his breath.

"A little filly."

Hannah and Todd entered April's stall and set their eyes on the prettiest thing they had ever seen.

Mrs. Marshall appeared at the stall. "I know you have a name picked out Hannah. You have been thinking on it for weeks."

Hannah smiled as she touched the fillies' soft nose, "I have thought and thought about it. Since April is her momma's name, I'm going to call her April's Lily. *Lily* for short. That is a lovely name, don't you think?"

"It is," said her mother.

"Catchy," said her father.

Hannah pet the filly some more, then reached up and rubbed April's long neck. April was tired, but proud to be a new mother.

Hannah jumped up and down in the thick straw of the stall. "I have to call Josephine! She'll be so excited to see her. She will love her!"

Hannah ran from the barn to the house, fumbling nervously as she dialed the telephone. Charlie Wilson answered

"Hello, Uncle Charlie! This is Hannah!" she said, trying to catch her breath. "I simply must talk to Jo right away!"

"I'm sure you must," he smiled as he handed the receiver to Jo.

"Jo, you have to come over now! " Hannah implored. "April just had her baby and I named her Lily. She is so cute!"

Jo hung up the phone and turned to her father. "April had her baby! A filly!"

Anne Wilson entered the kitchen. "What did she name her?"

"April's Lily," Jo said, grabbing a jacket.

"I'll drive," said her father.

"Can I bring Misha?" Jo begged her mother.

"I don't see why not. She's family."

Jo whistled and Misha came bounding into the kitchen.

Misha followed the family to the truck and jumped in. Jo tucked Misha between them as they drove off to the Marshall's red trimmed white barn.

Jo was so excited she had the door half open before the truck stopped running. She was inside the barn before her dad got out of the truck.

"Wow! Lily is beautiful!" Jo said as she touched the filly's soft nose.

Proud mother April turned and gave her filly a loving look with her large brown eyes. Lily had the same markings as her mother; A white star that went from the middle of the eyes down the nose and a good red sorrel coat.

Hannah and Jo settled in the fresh bedding on the stall floor to watch the pair and plan the future. Misha snuck in and sat by the door, curious at the sight of a newborn. That day a red sable border collie was as curious as the girls. Misha cocked her ears and watched with everyone as Lily stood on long thin legs for the first time. April gently nudged her with her nose as if to say, "You can do it."

"Look at those legs!" Hannah remarked. "She's a jumper, sure enough! I'll bet I could take her all the way to the Grand National in England if I trained her right!"

"England?" said Jo.

"Someday I'll tell you all about it," said Hannah.

Misha crawled on her belly through the straw and lapped at April's tired face.

"Will you look at that!" said John Marshall. "If that don't beat all."

CHAPTER 8

BREAKING IN LILY

The heat of summer turned to the fresh chill of autumn. The annual calf round-up at the Wilson and Marshall ranches only took a day. All the calves were accounted for and shipped off in big cattle trucks to be sold at auction to the highest bidder.

The cows didn't seem to miss their calves much after a few days.

Charlie Wilson was making more house calls than usual in town. Something he called "flu season" whenever he headed out the door with his black medical bag.

With the calves off the ranch, Hannah and her father John spent their spare time working with April's Lily in the exercise pen. The big round pen was covered with deep sand to cushion any quick jumps or leaps the young horse made and there were no corners for Lily or Hannah to get caught in.

Hannah had never trained a horse from birth before. Jo and Misha joined her after school sometimes to watch her progress with the feisty young filly.

"You have to teach Lily to trust and obey you first," said John Marshall as he showed Hannah how to put a halter on Lily. "You won't be able to ride her until springtime."

Hannah always spoke to Lily in a low soft voice before each training session. Her eyes met with Lily's big brown eyes in a moment of understanding so Lily would know what was expected. Hannah always reassured Lily by patting her on the neck while looking her in the eyes and using gentle slow movements.

Before each practice, Hannah would slide the halter over Lily's face and slowly move it over her ears and then gently bring the strip under her neck. Hannah would attach the halter next just below Lily's left ear with a snap hook. Hannah held the lead line attached to the halter under the chin in her left hand. With her right hand on the halter at April Lily's cheek, she would begin to walk slowly. Lily calmly followed Hannah's lead.

"Good girl," Hannah always said as they walked around the ring of the corral.

Jo always sat on a rail outside the corral with April tied to a post nearby to reassure Lily that all was well.

"A walk in the park,' Hannah called to Jo as she and Lily practiced. And it was pretty much a "walk in the park" for both of them as they circled around and around and around the circular pen.

Occasionally John Marshall would enter the corral and offer new advice to Hannah.

"Consistency is important," was at the top of the list of DO'S. "And if in doubt, DON'T," he'd say. "Some things are just plain hard to undo."

Hannah always remembered those two rules of training. She worked with Lily every day after school for thirty minutes and on the weekends an hour a day in the afternoon. By the end of the first year Lily would learn to be relaxed and at ease with a halter

Buck Fargo, the farrier who shoed all the horses for the Marshalls and Wilsons, commented on how calm and cool Lily was when she got new shoes every six weeks.

"She's got good balance," Buck said. He showed Hannah and Jo Lily's old shoes. "See how she wears 'em down? No hot spots."

"Would that help make Lily a better jumper?" asked Hannah.

"Yes," said Buck. "These shoes show she's coming down nice and flat all across. Kind of like a person jumping off a ladder. You don't want to land on just one toe and break it; you want to land flat with the whole foot for support. That's Lily for you."

Buck Fargo knew his business, the girls guessed.

Lily didn't shy away from the horse trailer either. She would step up and walk forward to be loaded. She also was a pro at backing out of the trailer without any stress.

Hannah had also worked with Lily by making noises and flapping objects at her to teach her not to be spooked. The first few times Hannah introduced a new and strange sound such as a waving hat or a rattling bucket of rocks Lily would jump and run away. In time however, Lily would just stand and look at Hannah. The look in her eyes was almost like saying, "Is that the best you can do to scare me?"

Because the young horse's bones and joints were soft and fragile, the ground work was limited to walking and lunging. To lunge, Hannah would hold a long lead line twenty-five feet long attached to Lily's halter. Then she would urge Lily to move in a large circle at three different paces - a walk, a trot, and a canter.

Hannah was impatient. She couldn't wait until next spring to climb on Lily's back for the first time.

"Lily will be a fine horse," Jo told her.

CHAPTER 9

THE BIG CAT IS BACK

Hannah called over her shoulder, "Jo is outside on Sundance and we are going to take the horses for a ride."

Todd, always ready to ride, yelled from the stairs. "I'm coming too."

Smokey, his brown marbled appaloosa gelding, needed to be ridden.

"Okay," Hannah yelled back. "See you at the barn."

Jo and Misha waited by the barn as Todd saddled Smokey and Hannah saddled April. Todd helped her put a halter on Lily.

"Looks like we're going for a real ride," said Jo.

"You bet," smiled Hannah with a twinkle in her eyes.

Todd waited for Hannah to jump in the saddle atop April and handed her the lead for Lily. He grabbed his saddle horn and pulled himself up on Smokey.

"I'm ready when you are, Hannah!"

The three waved goodbye to Mrs. Marshall as they rode through the barn gate. Misha trotted along next to Jo and Sundance, her eyes alert for any movement in the tall grass.

The horses walked a nice easy walk, reins in a smooth swinging beat under their heads. Once in a while eager Lily would trot ahead of April. Hannah gave her a gentle pull back on the lead line and she let April take the lead again.

They left the open grass and followed the hilly sloped trail into a forest of tall lodge pole pines and evergreens scattered with aspen and scrub oak. It was an old jeep road wide enough for two horses with twists and turns that hid the view ahead with tree limbs and scrub oak that billowed like balloons from their roots.

Some of the pine trees had low hanging limbs. The riders had to bend at the waist and lean their heads low to the saddle to avoid them.

Misha sensed something ahead and took the lead, darting between the moving horses' legs. She suddenly stopped, her happy frolicking forgotten.

The riders pulled their jumpy horses to a stop behind her, humans and animals sensing pending danger.

"What is it?" Jo asked Misha.

Misha turned to Jo, then back towards the trail ahead, her wet nose in the air, sniffing.

"The big cat must be back!" Todd said with a little panic in his voice.

There was a mountain lion that every few months would put this area on its course.

Hannah was having the hardest time keeping April and Lily calmed down. She kept changing hands that held the lead line that was attached to Lily's halter. Lily was anxiously crow-hopping, taking quick short little jumps like bucking but not with the force or height. Lily reminded Jo of a bird jumping on the ground for no good reason. Now April started rearing up to crow-hop, coming down hard on her front legs. One horse would have been a handful in itself but Hannah had two to deal with.

Jo did her best to hold Sundance back. He started going in circles, nickering and backing up, then going in circles again.

Todd did his best to rein in Smokey and keep him from galloping back to the ranch, forcing him in tight circles, pulling the right rein close to his knee.

If that wasn't enough excitement, the kids saw a flash of dull yellow crossing the path ahead of them and climbing a tree.

"The big cat is back!" Todd yelled.

"We see it!" said Jo.

Misha stood in the trail, paws firm in the ground, her red fur bristling at the sight of the mountain lion. She started to bark.

Lily suddenly turned in a half-circle, twisting the lead rope around Hannah, April and herself.

Hannah screamed, "I can't hold them!"

The tension on the rope came across her saddle and knocked her off. Then Smokey bucked high in the air and came down hard, tossing Todd to the ground. Sundance bucked high off his rear legs and threw Jo head over heels against Hannah as she fell.

The horses took off on a run back towards the ranch.

Jo, Hannah and Todd sat on the ground huddled together, eyes staring at the big cat in the tree.

Misha was still standing firm, eyeing the tree with warning barks.

Jo was the first to speak. "Hannah! Todd! Are you okay?"

Todd took off his ball cap and waved it at the big cat. "I'm okay. You?"

"I'm okay," Jo said. "Hannah?"

Hannah answered with pain in her voice. "I can't move my leg. I think I broke it."

Misha instinctively stepped forward, keeping herself between the kids and the tree.

Jo stood and put an arm under Hannah. She tried lifting her. "Try to stand up with me."

Hannah grabbed Jo's hand as she pulled her up. A sharp pain shot through her leg. Hannah groaned through clenched teeth.

"Todd, help me with Hannah!" Jo said.

Todd pulled himself up and put his arm around Hannah's waist on the other side.

"It's a long walk back home," Todd said.

"We can't just stay here," said Jo. "Not with that cat close by!"

They watched Misha, a low growl rising from deep within her as she continued to eye the tree that held the cat.

"I don't think that cat will come down from the tree if the three of us stay close together," Hannah moaned.

"And we have Misha!" Todd said.

"The cat doesn't know what to make of us," Hannah said.

"I remember what my dad told me," said Jo. "If we keep facing the cat he won't come at us."

"And then what?" said Todd.

"We have to walk backwards. As far away as we can," said Jo.

"What about Misha?" said Hannah.

"She'll move with us, you'll see," Jo said.

They started walking backwards, keeping their eyes on the dull yellow spot high in the green pine boughs.

Hannah lamented, "If that cat jumps down we're goners."

Jo answered, "My dad told me a mountain lion will usually stay treed with a barking dog below."

"I am so glad we brought Misha today!" said Hannah.

"She saved our lives, for sure," said Todd.

As the kids stepped backwards, Misha retreated with them, one cautious step at a time, always facing the treed mountain lion.

The three kept walking backwards for what seemed a mile. It was a slow march supporting Hannah one step at a time. Misha trotted behind them, turning every few feet to look up at other trees, letting out small barks as warnings.

It was a long, slow walk that seemed to last hours.

"We'll be lucky to make it home before dark," said Todd.

At last they were out of the sloping woods on the flat ground of prairie.

"I think it's finally safe to turn around now," Hannah said bravely.

Slowly they turned away from the hills. It was an easier walk, helping Hannah step forward. Misha stayed behind them, eyes cautiously glancing back to make sure the cat wasn't following.

"Good girl, Misha," the kids said one at a time.

When they reached the open pasture of the Marshall ranch the kids felt safe for the first time. Misha trotted alongside them now, knowing she had done her part.

"I have to rest up," Hannah said. "I can't walk another step."

The kids sat down to rest.

"Wish we had some water," said Jo.

"I'll be fine," said Hannah.

Todd stood up and fanned his hat across Hannah's face to cool her off. "The horses should be back home by now, as fast as they took off. Hopefully one of our dads will come looking for us. They should be home from work by now,"

Jo was thinking the same thing. The kids huddled together and waited. Misha sat a few feet away from them, facing the darkening forest behind them, her eyes wide and alert for danger.

As dusk turned to night they heard the sound of a truck.

A smile broke out on Todd's face. "It must be our dad!"

The sound became the lights of a the truck they all knew and loved. Even Misha seemed to have a bounce in her step.

John Marshall pulled up and stopped, the lights of the truck falling against three odd shapes and a dog.

"What the heck happened?" Mr. Marshall said.

"The big cat is back!" said Todd. "He almost got us if it weren't for Misha!"

Mr. Marshall walked over to Misha and knelt next to her, rubbing her tense body up and down to calm her. "That's a good dog," he said. "Good girl!"

"Dad, we are so glad to see you," Hannah said.

Jo helped her stand up and leaned her against the truck.

"What have we here?" Mr. Marshall said as he crossed to his daughter.

"My leg," Hannah said. "Feels like it's broken."

Her father opened the passenger door of the truck, picked her up and set her in the cab. "Try not to move it," he ordered. "Jo and Todd, climb in the back with Misha."

He jumped behind the steering wheel and turned the truck around. "We were worried sick about you three," he said. "Just glad you're alright."

He drove slowly to avoid ruts in the road, putting a firm hand on Hannah's leg to keep it from moving.

Misha leaned her head out of the back of the truck and looked at Hannah.

"I'm okay," Hannah told Misha. "Thanks to you."

Todd started singing a song he learned in 4-H. Jo and Hannah joined in. Mr. Marshall tried to sing along but he couldn't remember the words of the song from his youth. The kids laughed together and for a few minutes Hannah forgot about the pain in her leg.

When the truck pulled into the Marshall drive it was a comfort to see all the lights on in the house. Charlie and Anne Wilson were standing on the porch with Claire Marshall. They came down the steps and helped Hannah get out of the jeep.

"Slow as she goes," said John. "Hannah's got a gimped-up leg."

"Where are the horses?" Hannah asked.

"In the barn eating hay without a care in the world," said Mrs. Marshall.

Jo, Todd and Misha climbed out of the back of the truck.

"Sundance too?" said Jo.

"Sundance too," said her dad.

"Danged horses!" said Todd. "Scared of a little old mountain lion!"

Jo poked him. "You mean a *big old mountain lion*!"

The adults laughed nervously between them, aware that things might have turned out differently that day. They set Hannah on a hard wooden chair on the porch.

Misha raced between their legs, her tail wagging and barking her version of the Big Cat story.

Charlie and Anne Wilson hugged their daughter.

Claire Marshall hugged Todd close to her side. "You gave us such a scare, son."

"It was nothin' mom," said Todd.

His dad John came up behind him and hugged him next. "You still had us worried," he said.

The adults moved Hannah inside the house to the kitchen and sat her in a chair. Claire Marshall wrapped ice in a towel and set the ice pack on her daughter's leg.

"I'll grab my bag out of the truck and have a look at Hannah's leg," said Charlie as he headed outside.

Sometimes it paid to have a real doctor in the house.

Todd smelled chili cooking on the stove. "I'm near starved to death," he said.

"Would anyone else like a bowl of chili?" said his mom.

Hannah and Jo raised their exhausted hands.

"What about Sundance?" Jo asked. "Can we leave him here for the night?"

"Sure," said Mr. Marshall.

"You can leave Misha with us, too," said Todd.

Misha was curled up at Jo's side, eyes closed and breathing softly after an eventful day.

"No thanks. I think Misha deserves a good night's sleep in her own bed," said Jo.

Todd nodded as he dug into a hot bowl of chili placed before him.

Everyone laughed and laughed as food bowls were handed out.

Jo filled a big bowl with water and placed it in front of Misha. Tired Misha hung her head over it and slurped it up.

"That is some dog!" Todd said.

"Better than a turkey?" said Jo.

"Except on Thanksgiving," Todd winked.

Charlie returned with his bag and spent the next twenty minutes studying Hannah's leg. He gave her some pills to ease the pain.

Despite Hannah's mishap, the Wilsons and Marshalls were a happy family again.

CHAPTER 10

MISHA AND THE SNAKE

Hannah's leg wasn't broken. It was stiff and sore from two pulled muscles. She was glad that was the only problem as she wanted to start training Lily again.

For a couple of weeks she was content to lead Lily on walks in the pasture as she rode April. Once in a while she would get off April and lead both of the horses to give her own leg some exercise.

It was fun to ride with Jo, her best friend. She enjoyed having Misha along for company too.

Both girls knew to watch her and the horses. Animals always sensed anything new - from a squirrel scampering up a tree, to birds in bushes and especially the smell or sight of a mountain lion.

Misha loved going out on these outings. She chased anything that came along. Chasing a deer was her favorite.

"Misha is so fast! I bet she could catch a deer if she put her mind to it. She is like a brown pencil line when she runs. Do her feet touch the ground?" Hannah asked.

Jo just laughed.

On both sides of the trail wildflowers danced in the breeze. In another week they would all be gone.

Hannah and Jo named them as they rode.

Hannah pointed at yellow petals looking like large white daises but bright yellow.

"Nut tall sunflowers," she said.

Jo pointed at the white Colorado columbines scattered in a bed of purple wildflowers.

"They remind me of trumpets blowing," Jo said.

They rode through a field of mountain bluebells, their clusters of petals on long stems swaying in the breeze.

Jo sighed, "Isn't this a lovely trail this time of year?" She was talking more to herself than Hannah

Misha was full of high energy trotting between the legs of the horses determined to be in the lead.

"Misha not only runs fast but she is never tired," said Hannah watching Misha who by this time was the leader by some distance.

They had packed a sack lunch. The late spring weather just seemed to say, "Lunch on this ride".

They rode toward five odd-shaped boulders stacked on top of each other.

"What do they look like to you?" Jo asked Hannah.

"A big stack of puffy pancakes."

"I think they're pillows. Feather pillows. See the one at the very top?"

"Looks like a giant climbed up and sat on it," laughed Hannah.

There was an aspen grove to one side with yellow-petaled sneezeweeds pointing down and not up like the sunflowers along the trail. Everywhere Indian Paint Brush in reds and blues and wild poppies grew next to tree trunks.

"I think this is a beautiful place to have our picnic," said Hannah.

The girls dismounted, carrying their lunches and thermoses of lemonade with them. They set them down and removed the horse bridles, replacing them with halters on long lead lines so the horses could feed on the lush banquet of flowers all around.

The girls retrieved their lunches and pulled each other up the boulders, one pancake or pillow at a time until they settled on the top flat rock. They opened their sack lunches and spread their sandwiches, chips, and homemade chocolate chip cookies out on yellow paper napkins.

"I have a dream I want to share," Hannah told Jo.

"What is it?"

"I want to enter Lily in a jumping contest. Lily's legs are long enough for jumping. Do you know anything about the Grand National?"

"Not really," said Jo. "Just from that movie *NATIONAL VELVET* I watched with you."

"It's what they call a steeple chase. It was invented in England. They put out a bunch of rails at different heights and at different lengths apart. My job is to jump over them with Lily."

"You think Lily's ready?"

Hannah pushed up her ball cap. "She's almost as tall as her mother. She stands fifteen and a half hands now and she's still growing."

Jo's eyes caught Misha down below. She was sniffing around for a place to nap under a bush.

"So," said Jo as she opened her thermos. "Tell me more about the Grand National."

Hannah's voice was filled with excitement. "I really know a lot. The Grand National is a May race course in Liverpool, England. It is a cross country race over obstacles like hedges and walls and water. The horse and rider go twice around for a total of four and a half miles. It is the longest and hardest steeple race ever. A steeple race is a jumper race. Years ago, they used church steeples as landmarks. They still use the name. You know the English. So proper," said Hannah with a laugh.

"Really?" said Jo taking a bite of her turkey and cheese sandwich.

"Yes!" said Hannah.

"You have been doing your homework on this. I am impressed," said Jo.

"One more thing," said Hannah. "There are fifteen obstacles to jump and you jump them twice. The last two are the famous Chair and Water Jump. Those two you jump only once on the first time around."

"But first I would think you need to enter local and state contests here."

"Oh sure," Hannah said. "It takes a special saddle, too." She finished a bite from her sandwich and started on a cookie. "What about you, Jo? They have contests for dogs. We learned about them in 4-H."

"I know," said Jo. "I'm still doing my research."

The girls stayed up on the rock for a long time, talking and laughing and watching the horses grazing below.

Behind them, a fat bull snake slithered past to follow the warmth of the sun. Jo touched it as she reached for her thermos. She jumped up and screamed. Hannah jumped up and screamed. The horses jumped. Misha sat up in alarm and barked.

Jo shook her hand and arm as if the snake was still there. She saw his tail go over the side of the boulder. Talking fast and in a high voice she said, "A snake just slithered through my fingers."

"Where is he?" Hannah asked.

"Look!" Jo pointed her finger toward the ground. "I think that is him moving."

Hannah peered down at the grass. "It is a snake!"

The horses settled down again, watching the girls watching the snake.

Misha stood up and scampered in the brush around the boulder, sniffing the grass where the snake had just been. She turned and looked up at Jo, a crooked smile on her face.

"Looks like Misha chased the snake away," said Hannah.

"Good girl, Misha!" Jo said. She tossed a cookie to her and Misha chomped at her well-earned reward.

CHAPTER 11

THANKSGIVING

Thanksgiving was coming. The days of November were filled with a chill in the air. The pine tree branches were covered with snow that sparkled in the sunlight. The snow on the ground had a crunch in the shade and a softness in the sun.

In August Todd had taken first place in the 4-H Tom Turkey category at the county fair. Todd was so proud of the blue ribbon hanging on his bedroom wall. When he started his turkey project he told his parents that he wanted to raise a turkey from the egg to the plate. Now he wasn't so sure about his bravado.

Todd never admitted his affection to anyone but he had grown fond of big Tom. The curious turkey followed Todd around the pens, barn and corrals like a pet dog.

He asked his mom Claire about the unusual behavior of Tom one day.

"I can't shake him," complained Todd. "Sometimes when I go to feed the chickens, he runs up on them and chases them away. And you should see Tom when I saddle Smokey for a ride. He hops up on the fence and gobbles away with his wings flapping. He gets so mad like he's crazy."

"Tom isn't crazy," said Claire. "You're his mother. He's protecting you."

"His mother! Now why would Tom think that?"

"What was the first thing he saw when he hatched?"

"Me, I guess."

"Who fed him with an eyedropper when he was a chick? Who changes his water? Who feeds him?"

"Me," Todd realized.

"When Misha comes over with Jo, who locks Tom up in his pen to keep him safe?"

"Me."

"And if I recall, you taught Tom how to dig for worms."

"I had to. He didn't know how."

"And who gets all the dinner scraps?"

"The chickens mostly."

"And Tom," said Claire. "Don't think I don't see you giving him the lion's share."

"But I had to. He was my 4-H project and now..."

Claire sat with Todd to calm him down. "And now you're his mother and Thanksgiving is a week away and you don't want us to eat him. Am I right?"

Todd shrugged and kicked at the ground. "He's just a dumb turkey. I don't care for turkey much."

"Oh, you don't?"

"Never cared for it. I like chicken better. And I like ham better than chicken."

"What about prime rib?"

"I could eat that for Thanksgiving."

Claire hid a smile. "I hate all the fuss that goes with turkey. All those side dishes and the stuffing."

"Tom wouldn't be a good stuffer," said Todd. "If you plucked off his feathers, you wouldn't find much meat. Besides, I don't think he's big enough to feed a family."

"Which is why you suggest ham or prime rib."

"Makes sense," said Todd.

"Yes it does," said Claire. I'll talk to Aunt Anne and Grandma Elizabeth to get their opinions."

"Thanks, mom."

Todd nearly danced off to the barn to visit Tom. He was whistling off-key when he passed Hannah and Jo brushing their horses.

"Why are you so happy?" Hannah asked.

"I'm always happy," said Todd. He bent down and pet Misha. "You wanna come see Tom with me?"

Misha's ears perked up.

"Just kiddin'," said Todd.

At the Penner house Claire and Anne sat at the large kitchen table with their mother making cookies and pies.

"Look at us," smiled Grandma Elizabeth. "All covered in flour and sugar just like when you two were little!"

Anne laughed and sipped her hot tea.

Claire sifted colored sugar over a tray of unbaked cookies. "I know Thanksgiving is only a week away, but we have a situation," she said.

"Let me guess," said Anne. "The main course?"

Claire nodded. "Todd and Tom the Turkey are quite the pair now."

Anne smiled, thinking of Jo and Misha. "I can see how he would be attached to Tom. They have been together every day for almost a year."

Grandma Elizabeth added, "And we can't very well butcher a blue ribbon turkey."

"Exactly!" smiled Claire.

"I think we should have ham or prime rib," said Anne.

"That's fine with me," said Grandma Elizabeth. She shook her head. "You may not remember this because you were so young but Henry raised a turkey one year."

"What happened to it?" said Anne.

"He disappeared a week before Thanksgiving!" laughed Grandma Elizabeth.

"Disappeared?" said her daughters.

"In the back of his truck," laughed their mother. "I saw your father flying down the road with a trail of dust behind him. "Know what he said when he got back home and I asked him about it?"

"What?"

"Not a word. He didn't want to talk about it. That's a man for you."

"What should we tell our menfolk about Thanksgiving?" asked Anne.

"We don't have to say anything," said Grandma Elizabeth. "We're still in charge of our own houses."

Jo and Hannah came running in the door with Misha. They were out of breath from playing in the backyard.

Grandma Elizabeth wiped flour on her apron and turned to Hannah and Jo. "Girls, I want you to go out in the garage and take out the biggest ham we got in the deep freeze."

"What for?" said Hannah.

"I decided on ham for Thanksgiving at your house this year."

Jo and Hannah joined hands and danced around the kitchen.

When John Marshall arrived home from the feed store Todd met him outside.

"I did all the chores," said Todd.

"*All* of them?" said his father.

"I'm getting older now. It's about time I pitch in more."

"Thank you, son!" said John.

"Dad, I need to talk to you about something."

"What is it?"

"It's about that old turkey Tom."

"What about him?"

"I don't have the guts to butcher him."

"Oh!" his dad said rather importantly.

"I thought I could a year ago, but now he follows me everywhere. Mom thinks Tom thinks I'm his mama."

Mr. Marshall stroked his chin, thinking with a serious face on. "I understand your thinking, Todd. If you put the ax in my hand I couldn't do it either. But now we have a pickle. Thanksgiving is only a few days away. We'll need a great excuse."

"With a smile on his face, Todd suggested, "What if I start a turkey flock with Tom? I could sell the turkeys that I raise each year to other people."

His dad smiled. "Great idea!"

Father and son sat down on the porch, looking out over the land. His dad draped his arm over Todd's shoulder.

Todd shook his head. "I had a stomach ache all week seeing Tom on a large platter with vegetables around him."

They stood up when Claire and Hannah came towards them in the family car and parked by the house.

"Todd, help your sister with the groceries in the trunk. And John, will you grab that ham on the backseat?"

"Ham?" said John Marshall. "I thought we were having turkey for Thanksgiving."

"Grandma Elizabeth wants ham and ham it shall be," said Claire.

"Ham it is!" smiled John. He bent down and whispered in Todd's ear. "Funny how things just work out on their own sometimes."

Thanksgiving Day arrived. There was a wonderful mixed aroma in the Marshall house by the time the guests arrived. Even Misha was invited.

Anne brought freshly baked croissants made from Grandma Elizabeth's recipe and a pecan pie. Charlie brought a milk jug filled with homemade egg nog. Grandma Elizabeth and Grandpa Henry arrived with her famous pumpkin pie, cakes and cookies. Claire made sweet potatoes to go with the ham that was in the oven. A green bean casserole with mushrooms was cooking on the stove next to a butternut soup prepared by Hannah and Jo. Hannah was taking a cooking class in school and thought she would experiment with her family with Jo's help.

After an hour of appetizers and refreshments the Marshalls, Wilsons and Penners sat down around a table covered with a white table cloth and fall colored linen napkins. The ham was in the center of the table with bowls of sweet potatoes and green beans on either side

Everyone smiled as a family tradition started. One by one each family member rose from the table and shared what he or she was thankful for that year.

Grandpa Henry was thankful for another year of good health.

Grandma Elizabeth was thankful for a family that was close by and enjoyed each other.

Anne and Claire agreed with grandma about the family and they both got a little teary-eyed when they talked.

John and Charlie were thankful for their clients and that they paid their bills on time.

All laughed.

Hannah was thankful for Lily and couldn't wait to start jumping.

Jo thanked Misha for being her best friend on four legs.

Todd was the last to speak. When his time came he cleared his throat and stood up.

"I have been doing some research on presidents and turkeys." He said nervously.

Everyone smiled and listened.

"Rumor has it that President Lincoln was the first to pardon a turkey on Thanksgiving. Others say it was President Truman. As you may not know, every year it is a presidential tradition to pardon a turkey at Thanksgiving. I called the White House but the phone was busy. You know how the holidays are. So, on behalf of the President of the United States, I, Todd Marshall, do hereby pardon Tom the Turkey to a full life at our ranch." He picked up his water glass and asked everyone to stand for a toast to Tom.

The family stood and raised their glasses high in the air for Tom the Turkey.

Todd sat down again and stabbed at the ham at the center of the table with his fork.

"I'm starving! Who wants a slice of ham? It's absolutely delicious."

CHAPTER 12

THE CHRISTMAS PAGEANT

Woodmen Elementary School was a two room school house. One room was called The North Room and the other was called The South Room. The South Room had grades first, second, and third. The North Room had grades fourth, fifth, and sixth. A grand total of thirty students attended Woodmen Elementary.

There were two large pocket doors between the two rooms. Four large windows were on the east side of each room. These windows opened from either the top or the bottom with a twist lock in the center. Under the windows was a long counter top with shelves and two cupboards for books, art supplies and other needs for each class room.

Black chalk boards filled the walls on the north end of the North Room and the south end of the South Room.

Every student had his or her own wooden desk and chair attached permanently to the floor. The tops of the desks opened for personal things, books and papers.

Mrs. Prentice, who enjoyed the eccentric side of life, taught the primary grades in the South Room.

Mrs. Roberts, a more down to earth woman, taught the upper secondary grades in the North Room.

Besides regular classes, the school held a few events every year, the most important event being the approaching Christmas Pageant. All of the students participated.

Christmas time was a very special time at Woodmen Elementary School. The students in the upper grades made their parents sachets from oranges or apples and cloves. They would take whole cloves and stick them in the fruit to cover them completely. These would be placed in drawers or closets.

Moms loved them.

The younger primary students made birdfeeders. They would take pine cones and roll them in peanut butter and bird seed. They would attach a wire to the top in order to hang them from a tree in the yard. The students hoped the birds would get to them before the squirrel.

Not only were gifts made for parents starting in December but rehearsals began for the Christmas Pageant to be held the last Friday of school before Christmas break. The script was the time honored story of the birth of Jesus. The inn and the stable were made by someone years ago. It was refurbished every year with a little paint and glue.

Practice was held the last half hour of school every Thursday and Friday until the big performance. Every student was involved. There were no speaking parts except for the student who played the Angel of the Lord. By the time the first rehearsal was over everyone was in the mood for Christmas and counting the days.

At lunch the girls shared their brown bags of sandwiches and chips and compared to see who had the best homemade cookies. The school sold pints of milk for a nickel and many of the girls shared them too.

The first day of rehearsal, the students were assigned their roles in the pageant. The most excited student in the school was Sally Stroud. Besides her flair as an aspiring actress she also had a keen eye for directing.

"Hannah gets to play Mary this year!" she announced. "You will look so serene in your mom's blue bath robe and light blue scarf over your head!" she told Hannah.

Hannah laughed. "Serene? I never thought of myself as serene when I would rather be out riding."

Sally studied a paper before her. She had taken notes when the roles were assigned.

"Jo is the Angel of the Lord this year. Isn't that fabulous, Jo? You have the only speaking part in the production! That makes you the star of the show!"

Jo bowed her head. She didn't want the role but there was no way the teachers would let her back out. "What are you this year?" she asked Sally.

"I'm in the angel choir again. Suits me fine. So many of the other kids have no singing experience. I'll have to teach them their parts from the back row since I am the tallest. I also have the only solo!" She threw her hands up and rolled her eyes.

Todd came over to their table and took a cookie that was sitting in front of his sister. "Are you talking about the Christmas Pageant?" he asked.

"Yes we are," answered Sally. She glanced down at her notes. "You, Luke and Matt Turner are the Three Wise Men. Isn't that exciting?"

"We prefer to call ourselves The Three Kings," said Todd. He glanced over his shoulder. "Hey Luke and Matt. Come here." Luke and Matt joined him. "What do you prefer? Wise Men or Kings?"

"I will answer to either a wise man or a king. How about a Wise King?" said Luke with pride in his voice.

"What about you, Matt?"

Matt Turner stole a second cookie from Hannah's dwindling pile and swallowed it whole. "I'll be a Wise King too."

Sally studied her notes again. "Who plays Joseph this year?"

"Your brother Tyler."

"Oh yes!" said Sally.

Hearing his name, Tyler came over to the table. "Do you think I can wear dad's striped bathrobe?" he asked Sally.

"I'm not sure how it will hold it up," she said.

"Maybe I'll use bailing twine."

"That will work," said Sally.

Luke turned and smiled at Jo. "Congratulations on being the Angel of the Lord."

"Thanks," said Jo. She felt the milk in her stomach churning into butter.

Mrs. Prentice came in and announced lunch was over. "Look outside," she added. "It's snowing!"

After lunch came Social Studies with Mrs. Roberts in the North Room for the upper grades. The three students in fourth grade studied Colorado History. The four students in fifth grade studied United States History. The five students in sixth grade worked on drawing a map of South America.

While Mrs. Roberts discussed history with one grade, the other two grades worked on assignments at the chalk boards. It always amazed the students how Mrs. Roberts kept things straight and never lost her voice with all the talking she did.

Soon Social Studies were over and then there was a fifteen minute recess for both rooms.

"Put on your coats and hats," advised Mrs. Prentice. "There's plenty of snow out there! Don't slip on the steps. There's ice!"

Everyone bundled up and headed outside into the fresh air. The primary grades headed to the merry-go-round and teeter-totter together.

The girls in Mrs. Roberts' room stood in a circle trying to decide if they wanted to brush the snow off the swings and slide or just stand there talking and laughing.

Matt Turner picked up some snow and pressed it into the soft shape of a snow ball. He raised his arm and let it fly toward the girls. He and the other boys laughed.

Jo saw it coming and yelled, "Look out!" as she ducked her head down.

The snowball hit Hannah in the shoulder.

The battle was on between the girls and the boys of Mrs. Roberts' room for the remainder of the afternoon recess. Snowballs were made and sent flying into the air from both sides. Laughter and screams of delight were heard from the girls and boys with big smiles on their faces.

When the bell rang the students were caked with snow and their hair and gloves were wet. Cheeks were rosy on all the young faces as they marched inside.

Mrs. Prentice ordered her students to put their wet clothes over the steam radiators. "We can't have any of you die from pneumonia before the Christmas Pageant!"

The rest of the afternoon was spent on Mathematics and Science until the first rehearsal for the Christmas Pageant began. The accordion doors that separated the North from the South room were pulled open from the center to make one big room.

In the days ahead, Mrs. Roberts and Mrs. Prentice reminded all the students that everyone was important and was needed. The main reason there were so many rehearsals was to practice the hymns that they only sang once a year together. Most everyone except Sally Stroud had forgotten the words they had learned the year before and they were sure to be nervous the night of the big event.

"It would be a tragedy to forget your parts in front of family and friends," Mrs. Prentice said dramatically.

The dress rehearsal finally came. There was great excitement among the students. Schoolwork was forgotten and the whole afternoon was dedicated to the pageant. All of the children in the primary classes were excited to be in the choir.

Bathrobes, twine, wings made from coat hangers and cheese cloth were piled on desks.

The school janitor came in to the big open room and unscrewed all the desks from the floor to make room for the stage and folding chairs to seat the next day's audience.

Mrs. Roberts and Mrs. Prentice were all in a dither going over the singing parts for the individual groups of students. Mrs. Prentice sat at an upright piano tucked between the pocket doors.

"A hymn should be sung from the heart, not spoken from the tongue," reminded Mrs. Prentice.

The rehearsal was an unorganized disaster of missed cues and misplaced costumes. Before the students were dismissed for the day, the teachers gathered them all together for a final cheering up.

Sally Stroud was allowed the last word before the children were dismissed. “A bad final rehearsal is always a good sign that we will have an excellent performance tomorrow.”

“Who said that?” Todd asked.

“Mr. William Shakespeare himself,” said Sally with determination.

By late afternoon on Friday, all was ready. All the costumes and wings were placed in the coat hall for the upper grades.

At the front of the North Room there was a large dark blue piece of material covering all the chalk boards. A giant moon and shooting stars had been painted on it. The door of an inn and the stable were placed in front of the covered chalkboard with bales of clean straw and hay donated by the Wilsons and Marshalls spread across the small set.

The smells reminded Jo of her family barn and eased her anxiety.

The school janitor came in and arranged a small tier of steps behind the door of the inn for the choir to stand on. Inside the stable, two small stools were placed for Joseph and Mary to sit on and an empty manger stuffed with green hay was set between them.

Sally Stroud’s mother arrived with a beautiful doll wrapped in white cloth to symbolize the baby Jesus. To the right of the set, two palm trees made from 2x4’s and crepe paper were brought in by Sally’s dad.

Mrs. Prentice reminded the students playing shepherds that they were to stand in front of the trees.

Several students volunteered to help the school janitor bring in rows of rented folding chairs for the parents and families to sit on. They were arranged in neat rows all the way to the back wall of the South Room side.

An hour before the actual performance, Mrs. Prentice made sure all her sheet music was in order long before she needed to sit down and play. She begged with Mrs. Roberts for one last musical run-through with the students but there was no time left.

It was almost 7pm. Pageant time!

Cars and trucks arrived outside in the falling snow, delivering friends and families to the schoolhouse. As guests found their seats, they listened to the sounds of happy and excited school children preparing.

In the hallway that ran the length of the school house the young performers hurried into their costumes, pulling bathrobes over their clothes and wrapping white tea towels on their heads to resemble shepherds. Twine was wrapped around waists to keep robes from dragging and to keep the students from tripping on the hems.

Several volunteer moms pinned and tucked, combed hair and calmed nerves.

Luke, Matt and Todd had each made their own crown out of cardboard covered with tin foil.

After Hannah dressed as Mary she helped Jo put a white sheet over her head and tied it with a white silk ribbon around the waist. They both laughed as Hannah tried to keep the very large angel wings in place behind Jo's back.

Jo's mom had made the wings using two coat hangers for each wing and covered them in cheese cloth with glued silver braiding on the sides.

The angel choir made theirs the same way but they were smaller and more manageable wings.

When Anne Wilson arrived with her husband, she hurried up to Jo and Hannah to inspect her work. "I bought the cheese cloth on sale. I wasn't going to spend more than five dollars. I know the wings won't last after tonight. In fact I am surprised they are still in one piece."

"They fit great," Jo told her mom.

A few parents went around lighting candles and the overhead lights blinked on and off, a signal that the pageant was about to begin.

The audience settled in their seats and quieted down. The overhead lights went completely dark. The soft glow of candles set the mood of quiet anticipation.

The annual Christmas Pageant finally started.

Mrs. Prentice began playing *'It Came Upon a Midnight Clear'*. The angel choir came in singing the last two stanzas of the hymn as they found their places onstage. A few of the wings got bent as the little singing angels were in awe of everything as they walked in.

Someone stepped on a robe and a parent had to catch them from falling. But that was the only mishap. Soon the choir stood together in a row with Sally in the center since she had the only solo.

Next, the extras came in and took their seats at the small tables standing behind the door of the inn. A bright spot light was turned on and the big star above the stable glowed in the night.

As Mrs. Prentice played *'While Shepherds Watch Their Flocks By Night'* the shepherds dressed in bathrobes and white tea towels on their heads came in, tapping staffs made from pine tree limbs on the wooden floor.

After the shepherds were assembled by the palm trees Jo took center stage.

She said in a loud clear voice, "Do not be afraid; for behold, I bring you good news of great joy which shall be to all people. There has been born for you a Savior, who is Christ the Lord. And this will be a sign for you: you will find a baby wrapped in cloth and lying in a manger."

Jo walked to the side of the stage as Joseph and Mary came in to *'Oh Little Town of Bethlehem'*. As they settled in the manger, Sally Stroud sang her solo part of the hymn beautifully.

Her brother Tyler looked just like Joseph would look. Somehow the striped bathrobe made it possible. Hannah in her mom's blue bathroom made her look serene and just how Mary would have looked. She carried the baby Jesus just as a mother would and placed the doll in the manger ever so carefully to make sure the baby sat high enough for the audience to see.

The Three Wise Kings arrived next carrying their gift boxes of gold, frankincense and myrrh wrapped in shiny paper. Todd, Matt, and Luke looked distinguished wearing their bathrobes and tin crowns. As they set their gifts beside the baby Jesus the choir sang '*We Three Kings of Orient Are*'. When the song ended, the three kings stepped away from the manger and stared up at the bright star shining above, their hands cupped together in praise.

Sally started singing '*Silent Night*' with the choir and gestured for the audience to sing along. One by one, friends and family joined in until the room was alive with music.

At the close of '*Silent Night*' the house lights went up. The show was over.

Clapping erupted from proud parents, friends and older brothers and sisters. The students took bow after bow for being great performers for one night.

After the performers removed their garments and dressed for the cold outdoors, homemade candy popcorn balls wrapped in clear cellophane tied with red ribbons were distributed by volunteer moms at the doorway.

It was snowing outside and the sights and smells of Christmas were in the air.

Mrs. Roberts and Mrs. Prentice stood in the cold outside wishing everyone a "Merry Christmas" as they received thanks for their excellent work with the children for another year.

As Jo walked to the family station wagon with her parents, she heard Misha's bark.

"You didn't leave her out in the cold this whole time!" Jo complained as she opened the back door.

Misha leapt out of the station wagon wearing a hastily attached wool blanket fastened with big bobby pins on her back.

"We tried to bring Misha inside," her dad explained, "but the janitor said she might bark and ruin the pageant."

Jo knelt down in the snow and patted Misha. "Our first Christmas together! Merry Christmas, little girl!"

Misha licked her face, ignoring the sweet smell of the candy popcorn ball in Jo's hand.

As the Wilsons drove out of the parking lot, they stopped to admire the tree decorated with lights standing in the snow in front of the school.

"What do you think?" said Anne Wilson.

"It's beautiful," said Jo.

She looked at the expression on Misha's wondering face. Misha thought it was beautiful too.

CHAPTER 13

THE STOCK SHOW

It was a family tradition to visit the big Denver Stock Show in mid-January every year and this year was no different. The Wilsons and the Marshalls always looked forward to their weekend together and there was so much to see and do.

It was only Wednesday, but the show was the only thing on Jo's mind as the school bus moved slowly down the dirt road crunching the snow under its tires as it went along. A cold wind with beads of hard snow blew hard against the bus windows, leaving a thick frost.

Hannah nudged Jo sitting next to her. "What are you thinking about?"

"What else?" Jo grinned.

"Just think! In two days we will be going to the Stock Show! I'll bet our prize bull Curly wins a ribbon this year! His coat is all shiny from those raw eggs dad gives him in his grain very day. This is the only time of year he gets treats on a daily basis."

Jo rolled her eyes. "I know about raw eggs. My dad gives them to his reining horse Bell when they compete."

Todd and Luke came up from the back of the bus and sat behind them.

"Wish I could go," Luke said. "I've never been to a big stock show. I'll be stuck in school while you three are eating corn dogs, fries and cotton candy. How many days do you get to skip?"

"I'm leaving tomorrow with my dad and Curly," Todd said. "My dad says it takes a day for a big bull to get adjusted to the commotion. We have a stall and I have to keep Curly clean and pretty."

Luke turned to Jo. "When do you leave?"

"Friday morning."

"Curly is sure to win a ribbon," said Hannah. "Maybe Best of Show! He's fat and sassy and will amaze the judges with his swagger when dad leads him in to the show ring."

"Curly sure is a big bull," said Luke. "I'll bet if we tried roping him he'd drag us all the way to the top of Pikes Peak."

"And then some," laughed Todd. "Curly breeds great calves. Hopefully the judges will see that in his bloodlines and conformation. But his isn't the best event this weekend."

"What is?"

"The indoor rodeo that kicks off the show. You should see all the cowboys, clowns and horses."

"They have barrel racing, too," Hannah added.

"I don't care about that," said Todd. "For me it's all about the cowboys."

"Roping too?" said Luke.

"Yep," Todd said. He crossed his arms and leaned back in his seat to dream with his eyes closed.

"What other events are there?" Luke asked Hannah and Jo.

"Blue ribbon competitions for other farm animals," said Hannah. "Chickens, ducks, rabbits, pigs, sheep, even goats."

"Some people sell their livestock at the show," said Jo.

"Those auctioneers talk so fast, I can't understand a word of it," said Hannah. "We also get to see jumping horses, dressage, halter and reining competitions."

Luke shook his head sadly. "Sure wish I was going."

Jo wiped the frost off the bus window and looked out at the falling snow. "There is something magical about the Stock Show," she said wistfully.

"There is," added Hannah.

"Oh, brother!" Todd said. He opened his eyes and turned to talk to Luke. "Let's talk about something else before the girls start yapping about buttons and bows."

"Like what?" said Hannah.

"Luke's stopping by our place with us. We got a science experiment."

"What is it about?" Hannah asked.

"We're going to make a hurricane in a plastic bottle," said Luke.

"How?' said Hannah.

"Easy. We fill half the bottle with water then we use a funnel, dump in some baking soda and screw the top back on the bottle."

"Doesn't sound like much of an experiment," said Hannah.

"Next we shake the bottle up and wait," said Todd.

"Wait for what?" said Jo.

"The chemical reaction," said Luke.

"What sort of chemical reaction?" Jo said.

"It's supposed to explode," said Todd.

Hannah shook her head. "You better not do it in the kitchen. Mom will tar and feather you."

"I got a spot picked out in the barn," Todd said nonchalantly.

"What if it catches on fire?" said Jo.

"It won't," said Todd. "We're using water. Remember?"

"Oh," realized Jo.

"Sounds like a dumb experiment," Hannah scoffed.

"That's because you didn't think of it," said Todd.

Hannah turned back in her seat and slunk down low with Jo so the boys wouldn't interrupt them again.

"We get a three day weekend!" she smiled.

"I love how it starts," said Jo. "My mom comes into my room to wake me. It is still dark and the windows have frost on them. The stars and moon are shining through the window. I can hear the radio playing in the kitchen. Dad is listening to the stock report, writing down the price of hay and feed. For some reason I never hear it on school days. Maybe he turns it up loud just for me. But that's not the best part before the stock show."

"What is?"

"It's the hot chocolate we drink driving to Denver. The smell and the steam that circle my face always make me smile."

"What about Misha?" said Hannah.

"My dad called Mr. Wills, the man we bought her from. He volunteered to feed the animals and look after Misha while we're gone."

The bus came to a stop and Todd was the first one out the door, pulling on his gloves as his feet hit the ground. He grabbed a handful of snow, turning it into a tight ball as he ran away from the bus.

"Hey girls - catch!" he said. He threw the snow ball and hit Jo squarely on the shoulder.

"You're going to get it now, Todd Marshall!" Jo said as she quickly patted snow into a ball and ran after him.

Luke got off the bus and as he ran to catch up with Todd he scooped up snow and dumped it on Jo as he raced past.

Jo stopped in her tracks, squirming from the cold snow trickling down her neck. She helplessly turned to Hannah, a furious expression on her face.

"I can't believe it!" Jo muttered between clenched teeth. "Luke put snow down my back!"

Hannah stepped behind her and brushed the remaining snow off Jo's neck. She was smiling.

"You're supposed to be my best friend," said Jo.

"I am your best friend," said Hannah.

"Then why are you smiling?"

"Because I think Luke likes you."

"*Likes me*?" said Jo.

"Sure," said Hannah.

"Boys are crazy," Jo said as they walked up the lane together, the boys far ahead of them by now.

"We'll never understand them," Hannah admitted.

"Never?" said Jo.

"Probably never," Hannah laughed.

Early Thursday morning before sunrise, John and Todd Marshall loaded Curly into his own personal stock trailer. Mrs. Marshall and Hannah watched as they drove down the road, their headlights showing the snow on the road.

An hour later the Wilsons came by the ranch with Mr. Wills and helped Claire feed the roaming cows and calves in the pasture. Charlie drove the truck slowly in a long straight line as Mr. Wills, Anne and Claire threw hay out the back of the tail gate.

A handful of curious hungry cows and calves trotted up to the long line of green hay lying on the snow and started eating.

When their chores were finished, Claire Marshall poured coffee for her volunteers in the kitchen. Hannah came in, carrying her school books. Her aunt Anne introduced Hannah to Mr. Wills.

"This is the man who gave Misha to Jo," added Uncle Charlie.

"How is Misha doing?" asked Mr. Wills.

Hannah talked for a minute about all the great adventures she and Jo had with Misha.

Mr. Wills was very pleased.

Hannah asked her uncle, "Can I catch the bus at your place with Jo?"

"Sure," said uncle Charlie.

Before Hannah climbed into the Wilson's truck she turned to her mom. "It is going to be very quiet tonight without Todd to take up all the dinner conservation."

Her mother just smiled.

When they arrived at the Wilson house, Jo and Misha were outside playing in the snow.

Misha recognized Mr. Wills when he stepped out of the truck and ran to him, hopping up and down, licking at his knees and gloves.

Jo watched with just a small hint of jealousy.

Mr. Wills walked up to her, Misha diving in between his legs as he stepped.

"Easy, Misha!" said Mr. Wills. "You got Jo to look after you now."

Misha returned to Jo's side and barked happily.

"Thanks for helping us with the animals," Jo said to Mr. Wills.

He put his hands on his hips and studied the ranch. "Heck of a place you have here, Jo. Dog heaven, I'd say."

Misha barked.

"See? Misha agrees with me," said Mr. Wills.

Hannah came up to Jo. "You ready for school?"

"Let me grab my books."

A minute later the girls were walking towards the road to catch the school bus.

Jo looked back for Misha. She was following Mr. Wills and her parents towards the barn.

"I won't see Misha for two whole days!" Jo pouted.

"She'll survive," said Hannah.

At school Hannah and Jo had a spelling test in English. They talked about U.S. history and learned about photosynthesis in science class. They shared their homemade lunches at noon.

The day seemed to never end. But at last the clock ticked "three". The bus was waiting outside to take them home.

The next morning, instead of pulling the covers over her head, Jo bounded out of bed like a rabbit. She pulled on her jeans, red plaid flannel shirt, and wool socks. She could smell something good coming from the kitchen and heard the familiar sounds of the radio broadcasting the morning stock report.

"Good morning, princess," said her dad as she entered the kitchen.

He was sipping coffee and reading a newspaper, just like Jo had imagined he would.

"Good morning, dad," Jo said. She sat down at the table. Her mom was at the stove, stacking warm pancakes on a plate.

"You awake yet?" her mother asked.

"I think so," said Jo.

Misha trotted up to her, the sound of her nails clicking on the wooden floor. She set her head in Jo's lap for a morning pet.

"I wish we could take her with us," said Jo.

"Misha will be fine," said her mom. She placed the plate of steaming hot pancakes topped with melting butter in front of Jo.

Jo picked up a bottle of syrup and dressed the pancakes. "I love how you put the butter on the pancakes at just the right temperature so it melts in the syrup," Jo said. "I told Hannah to tell Aunt Claire she needs to learn how to make pancakes like you."

"Oh, you girls!" Anne said. "You're just like twins."

Mr. Wills arrived at the kitchen door, dressed in overalls, cowboy boots and a big felt cowboy hat. Anne invited him in and poured him a big mug of hot coffee.

"A nice cold day," decided Mr. Wills as he finished his cup. He looked down at Misha waiting by the door. "Mind if Misha helps me with my rounds?" he asked Jo.

"She loves to help," said Jo.

"Come on, Misha," he said, opening the back door. "Let's see how much Jo taught you about being a cow dog."

Jo finished her last bite of pancakes and helped her mom wash the dishes. Finished, Anne took off her kitchen apron and hung it on a peg.

"Let's get going," she said. "Claire and Hannah are waiting for us to pick them up."

"You packed yet?" said Mrs. Wilson.

"Since Monday," said Jo.

"Toothbrush?"

"And soap and shampoo."

"That's my girl," said her dad. He picked up their suitcases. "I'll warm up the station wagon."

Jo hurried to pull on her winter boots and thick barn coat. She pulled her ball cap snug on her head and stuffed her gloves in her pocket. "I'm ready."

Anne filled a large thermos with the hot chocolate that the girls loved. Jo grabbed extra cups. The station wagon was pulled up to the house. Her father was ready to go. Mr. Wills came up from the barn with Misha at his side.

Jo bent down in the snow and patted Misha on the head. “You be a good girl,” she said. Jo looked at Mr. Wills. “Most of the time when I’m gone Misha likes to curl up in the hay with Sundance in the barn.”

“I’ll make a note of that,” smiled Mr. Wills.

Misha wagged her tail and trotted off to the barn.

Mr. Wills laughed. “Looks like she’s ready for her first nap of the day!”

When the Wilson station wagon pulled up to the Marshall house, Hannah came out carrying her overnight bag. She wore a blue wool sweater and jeans. Her mom was right behind her with an enormous suitcase. They tossed their bags in the back of the station wagon and climbed in the back seat with Jo.

Charlie Wilson shook his head. “You sure you brought a big enough suitcase Claire?”

“Oh, go on with you Charlie!” she laughed.

He shook his head again. “Women and their ways. It’s a mystery!”

He shifted gears and they were off to the Denver Stock Show.

When the station wagon reached the highway, Anne asked, “Is anyone ready for hot chocolate?”

Both girls smiled and said, “Yes, please.”

Anne opened the thermos, poured the wonderful liquid into the cups and passed them out.

As the steam and smell encircled Jo’s face she whispered to Hannah, “Isn’t this magical?”

“Just like you said it would be!” Hannah whispered.

The girls smiled as they sipped the hot chocolate.

The sun was coming up over the eastern horizon. The skyscrapers of Denver were soon in their sights as the station wagon reached the top of a long hill that revealed the city basin below.

"It sure is a big town!" Jo said.

"Too big for my liking," said her father.

Past downtown Charlie turned off the highway and followed the large red STOCK SHOW signs and arrows to a large parking lot filled with pickups, trailers, and cars.

The air was cold and crisp. Jo could see her breath when she climbed out of the back seat of the station wagon. Hannah buttoned her coat and put her gloves on.

"Where to?" asked Claire as she grabbed a small camera from her luggage.

Charlie pulled out an envelope from his back pocket that held the tickets for the events.

"Bull Barn Number 1."

With smiles and laughter, they headed off to find John and Todd.

The barn inside was a large open space. Walkways separated the rows of fenced in bulls from each other. The concrete floor was covered with clean straw for bedding. Each bull had two buckets. One for feed and one for water.

The proud bull owners helped each other out by cleaning the piles of manure in the walkways. If an owner went off to get lunch or watch an event, someone always volunteered to watch his bull.

All the bulls wore halters, their lead ropes attached to a large metal ring on the wall or tied to the railing if they were in the open areas. Big as they were, the bulls seemed friendly. They had been groomed and were accustomed to people for months if not years.

These were more than pasture bulls. They were show bulls worth their weight in gold for the blood lines that they passed on.

Since it was Curly's first show, both families were excited and eager to see how he would do.

"I see my dad and Todd," Hannah said. She waved her arms high in the air towards them. Todd saw them and jogged over to meet them.

"How was the drive?" Todd asked Hannah and Jo.

"Great," Jo answered thinking of the hot chocolate.

Todd pointed at his dad. He was brushing down Curly. Curly was in cow heaven.

"I learned a lot on the trip with dad," Todd told Hannah as he led everyone forward.

"Like what?" Hannah said.

Todd went on. "Dad and I were talking to some of the old timers. Did you know there are over twenty breeds of cattle? When the stock show started in 1906 there were only four breeds. Registered Herefords, Black Angus, Galloway and Shorthorns. We're raising one of the foundation breeds. How cool is that?"

John Marshall set down his brush and kissed his wife on the cheek. He had a big smile on his face. "Curly's getting a lot of attention," he said. "I think we got a winner."

"What time is Curly's event?" Charlie asked.

"11:00 o'clock," said John.

Charlie looked at his watch. "We have plenty of time to check the other cattle barns, the sheep and goats."

John turned to the rancher in the next stall. "Mind keeping an eye on Curly for a bit?"

"Not at all," said the rancher.

The Wilsons and Marshalls wandered up and down the aisles of Bull Barn #1 and entered Bull Barn #2.

"I never saw so many bulls in one place!" said Todd.

The time passed quickly as the family visited the sheep and goat barns.

John looked up at a large clock on the wall. It said 10:30. "We should be heading back. I want to do a final checkup on Curly before we move him to the arena."

With that, the merry band headed to bull barn #1.

John and Todd gave Curly a final brushing and made sure his tail was clean, especially the white at the tip. Curly looked handsome as any bull could. John untied the lead rope, turned Curly around and led him to the arena. Curly's tail was swishing like a dog as he walked next to John. He was one proud bull, his head held high. Even though it was Curly's first competition, he was acting like an old pro.

As John and Curly approached the gate to the arena the others handed their tickets to the attendant and hurried to their seats. Front row of course. Curly and John's big day had finally arrived.

John and the other ranchers walked the bulls around the arena three times while the judges scribbled notes. There were fifteen bulls competing for the three top places.

Finally the ranchers and their bulls lined up and faced the judges. Each rancher made sure his bull was standing "square," the back feet and the front feet in a straight line so their shoulders and back were straight.

The judges walked in and out between the standing bulls taking more notes.

Jo, Hannah and Todd watched intently, their arms resting on a top railing, their chins on their hands; they were giving their full attention.

The judges finished their inspection and huddled together over a big folding table, talking in hushed voices as they compared notes.

"What are they doing?" asked Jo.

"Voting for the top three bulls," said Todd.

One of the judges stood up and took a long glance at Curly again before he wrote down his vote on a piece of paper and handed it to the Ring Announcer.

The announcer took a minute to tally the votes and walked up to a microphone.

"Here it comes!" said Aunt Claire. She crossed her fingers for luck.

The announcer spoke in a big booming voice. "The judges have made their final decision. I am happy to announce the third place winner..."

Jo, Hannah and Todd held their breath.

"Will Mr. Edwards and Number 11 please come forward?"

Mr. Edwards stepped forward with his bull. He shook the judges' hands and received a third place white ribbon.

The announcer spoke again. "Mr. Smith and Number 9, please come forward for the second place ribbon."

Mr. Smith came forward with his bull and was awarded a red ribbon. One by one the judges shook the owner's hand.

Jo glanced over at Aunt Claire and her parents. They were leaning forward, holding their breath like the kids.

After a long and dramatic pause, the announcer said, "Will Mr. Marshall and Number 6 please come forward. Congratulations! You have won the blue ribbon."

Uncle John stepped forward with Curly. Jo had never seen such a big grin on her uncle's face.

The announcer handed Uncle John the beautiful blue ribbon. "Well done! This is your first competition at this level isn't it?"

"Yes it is," Uncle John said with a huge smile.

"Well deserved, sir."

The judges came forward and congratulated Uncle John.

The Marshalls, Wilsons and everyone in the stands stood up clapping and whistling.

"He won!" Aunt Claire shouted with a sigh of relief.

"Look at old John pumping those hands," laughed Charlie Wilson. "You'd think Curly just got elected president!" He put his fingers between his teeth and gave a loud whistle. "Way to go, John!"

Claire looked at Todd. "Congratulations, son. You played a big part in this, too."

Todd blushed.

"Well, you did!" said Hannah.

Everyone left their seats and met Uncle John and Curly at the arena gate. Uncle John was still smiling from ear to ear. Curly seemed to walk with a swagger, his tail swinging in beat.

"Dad, I am so excited for you", Hannah said. She gave him a hug.

Claire kissed her husband on the cheek.

Uncle John hugged Todd by the shoulder. "We did it, son! We did it!"

Todd turned to Curly and rubbed his big head. "Attaboy!"

The Wilsons stepped forward and gave their congratulations followed by a slew of strangers, some of them handing Uncle John their business cards.

As Uncle John led Curly back to Bull Barn #1, he said, "Let's get Curly put up and find ourselves the best steak in the place! It's time to celebrate. Like Grandpa Henry always says, 'You can't go wrong with cattle. America loves a good steak.'"

After Curly was back in his pen, the Marshalls led the Wilsons to one of the large pavilions. There was a variety of temporary restaurants to choose from tucked between booths selling everything cowboy imaginable including western hats, boots, shirts, pants, string ties, belts and buckles.

Hannah found a shop specializing in riding gear. "Look dad! This is what jumpers use!"

Uncle John picked up a small English saddle. "Think this might work for Lily?" he said.

"Maybe," said Hannah.

"I'll look into it later," he said.

At the end of the long corridor, Uncle John found a place serving steaks and hamburgers.

"Looks like we found something for everyone," he said.

The Marshalls and Wilsons found a long table near the back. The adults ordered steaks. The kids ordered open-faced hamburgers smothered in chile and cheese.

"You want chips with the burgers?" asked the waitress.

The kids nodded.

While they waited for their order, Claire studied a program. "There's so much to see!" she said.

Todd was anxious to see the rodeo on Saturday. "I went by the bucking stock this morning," he said. "They look tough."

"And the team roping tomorrow?" said his dad.

"That too!"

Hannah wanted to see the horse jumping that started in an hour.

Jo didn't care what she saw. At every turn there was something exciting to see.

"Do you know what the most exciting event in rodeo is?" Todd asked everyone.

"What is it?" said Hannah.

"Bull riding," Todd said. "It's the most dangerous eight seconds in a cowboy's life."

Their meals arrived. No one was shy about eating. Todd dumped a spoonful of chile into his mouth.

"I'll cheer for the bull," said Jo. "I love it when they do those spins with fire coming out of their eyes while the clowns rush in to save the cowboys when they hit the ground."

"Oh, Jo! How could you be for the bull?" said her mom. "I like the barrel racing with those fast quick horses sliding around those barrels, their female riders hanging on for dear life."

"Team roping is harder and requires perfect timing. Team roping is where it's at," Todd said stubbornly.

By the time they had finished their meal the horse jumping was starting. John Marshall paid the tab.

The arena where Curly had won his blue ribbon was rearranged with jumps in a varied pattern. Each jump was five feet high.

"I got the tickets," Uncle John said. "Front row." He reached into his side pocket and handed them to an attendant.

The first horse and rider entered the arena. Hannah sat up straight to get the best view possible. "Someday that will be me on Lily and then on to the Grand National."

Jo replied, "Yes you will. Just like Misha will be the best herding dog ever."

Hannah smiled and hugged Jo. "You're the best! I love you."

It was exciting watching the horses and their riders wearing British breech pants, jackets and small helmets as they made the turns and took their jumps around the arena.

"So elegant!" said Hannah.

Jo agreed.

Todd sat back in his seat, pretending he wasn't interested.

At last the event ended and the winners were announced.

The Wilsons and Marshalls headed back to check on Curly. Several breeders and ranchers had stopped by looking for Uncle John.

"You all go on to the hotel. I'll stay here for the night with Curly," he said. He pointed to a small folded cot in the corner.

"I'll stay too," said Todd.

"No, you go on with the others," said his dad, "while I make some breeding deals for Curly."

"The hotel has an indoor heated swimming pool," said Claire.

"Really?" said Todd.

"I never heard such a thing!" said Mrs. Marshall.

The Wilsons and Marshalls drove to their hotel and checked in. They had adjoining rooms. While the kids played in the swimming pool, Charlie went down the street and returned with two large pizzas and cold soda pops for everyone.

Charlie found a new television show called *GUNSMOKE* on the black and white television and the family settled in to watch it. By the time the episode ended, Jo, Hannah and Todd were sound asleep on the floor, pillows tucked under their heads. Anne and Claire woke them up and the kids crawled to their big fluffy beds to sleep.

"Are you tired?" Anne asked Jo as she pulled the covers up.

"Bushed," said Jo.

In less than a minute Jo was sound asleep again.

The adults stayed up a little longer playing gin rummy at a table.

"I wish I was a kid again," said Charlie.

"It's the best time of life," said Claire.

"Magical," said Anne.

Todd was up at dawn, shaking Jo and Hannah from their sleep. The kids sat on the floor playing Go Fish with a deck of cards until they heard their parents stir and rise.

They all walked down to the hotel restaurant and had their fill of pancakes, bacon and eggs. After breakfast the kids decided to swim in the pool again before they checked out and drove back to the stock show.

Anne filled her thermos with hot black coffee and Claire bought a bag of pastries for Uncle John.

When they arrived at Curly's pen, Uncle John was sitting on a stool next to the shiny Blue Ribbon posted on the fence. A stack of business cards bulged in his pocket.

"I didn't know sleeping in a barn with a bull could be so profitable!" he laughed.

Todd was anxious to see the afternoon rodeo. John handed him their tickets and Todd led everyone to the arena.

The entire audience stood as The National Anthem played.

The first events were the saddle bronc, bare-back bronc and barrel racing. The half time show followed with a woman holding a jump rope doing tricks with dancing little dogs. Clowns in a small cart pulled by small ponies came out next and entertained the audience when the wheels fell off the cart and they tried to fix it.

Before the team-roping event started, Hannah and Jo ran off to buy peanuts and cotton candy.

Todd couldn't take his eyes off the team-ropers. Jo had never seen him sit so quietly as he watched the horses, the cowboys and the steers. He played close attention to the cowboys doing the heeling, coming up after the running cows to snag their hind legs with a rope.

"Wow! Did you see that catch?" Todd said to anyone who might be listening.

His father answered, "He was amazing. That loop was laid down right in front of the back feet and tightened so fast."

"That's my goal," Todd added. "Quick and accurate."

The bullriding was the last and most exciting event.

Two rodeo clowns strolled into the arena with a barrel open on both ends. While they poked and jabbed at each other the announcer said over a loudspeaker, "Out of chute number 3 is Sky Rocket ridden by Andy Hayes."

Andy Hayes lasted three jumps and four seconds. He was on the ground with the bull bearing down on him.

The clowns went into action. One jumped in the barrel and the other one rolled it between the bull and Andy. The bull stopped, stared down at the barrel and lowered its head.

Andy Hayes got up, ran to the chute railing and climbed up to safety. The bull started pawing the ground and pushing the barrel around with its head. After he stopped and walked away the clown in the barrel stood up in the barrel and waved at the bull. Just then two pickup riders rode up between the bull and the clown, their lassos flying in the air as the bull was snagged led back to the catching pen.

"I love it!" Jo said, clapping.

She sat back in her seat and waited to cheer on the next bull as it bucked and twisted with "fire in its eyes."

"It looks so scary to me," Hannah said.

"And dangerous," said Todd. "That's what makes it fun."

The last bull, Raging Thunder, bucked all the way across the arena with a cowboy on its back. That cowboy did make the eight seconds. He jumped off the bull onto the back of one of the pick-up men's horses and rode off to safety while the mad bull was led into the catching pen.

The cowboy slid to the ground, took off his hat and waved to the crowd.

"Looks like we got a winner," said Todd. He poked at Jo. "And it wasn't your bull."

The announcer said, "Thank you all for coming this afternoon. Give the cowboys and the stock a round of applause. They are all athletes."

The audience gave a thundering hand-clapping whistling foot stomping response.

The Wilsons and the Marshalls gathered up their belongings and headed back to the bull barn. It was time to get Curly and head home.

Curly was contently eating hay when they all walked in. Todd raked up the straw bedding, Hannah cleaned out the hay barrel and Jo emptied Curly's water bucket. Uncle John untied the lead rope and led Curly towards the large open door facing the parking lot.

Everyone gathered at the truck and stock trailer. Todd unlatched the gate and opened it wide. Uncle John led Curly in and secured the lead rope, patting him on the rear as he walked out. Todd closed the gate and made sure it was locked down for the ride home.

Charlie Wilson fetched his station wagon and unloaded the Marshall's bags into the truck. Aunt Claire held up the Blue Ribbon one last time for everyone to admire.

"Oh, I almost forgot!" said Uncle John. He went to the cab of his truck and lifted out a brand new English riding saddle for Hannah. "Think this will fit?"

Hannah took the small saddle in her arms. She was speechless.

"I'm a roper. Todd's a roper. You were born to be a jumper," said Uncle John.

Hannah's mother handed her a small riding crop and a leather hat with a brim. "I saw these in that movie *National Velvet*."

"Just like the Grand National!" Hannah stuttered. She handed Todd her new equipment and hugged her parents. "Thanks, mom and dad. It's the best gift *ever*!"

It was dark and the stars were shining when the Wilsons pulled down the road toward the house and barn. Mr. Wills came out of the barn, his overalls dirty, removing his work gloves to wave. Misha was at his side and she quickly trotted up to the station wagon. Jo got out and ran to give Misha a hug.

"Oh, what stories I have to tell you, sweet girl."

Misha followed her into the house. Jo sat by the burning fireplace Mr. Wills had started earlier. Misha curled up next to her.

Mr. Wills came inside with Charlie and Anne and they joined them.

"How did it go?' Mr. Wills asked.

"John's bull Curly won the Blue Ribbon," said Anne.

"That's real nice," said Mr. Wills. He looked at Jo. "Misha's one heck of a cow dog," he said, "but when she runs out on the pasture, she can't hear her commands so I got you something."

He handed Jo a small box and she opened it. Inside was an egg shaped metal whistle, shaped flat near the mouthpiece.

"It's a cow whistle. Comes with instructions. A dog can only hear you so far, especially in the wind and rain. Your voice can't be heard and Misha may not be able to see your arm commands. A whistle can be heard in any kind of weather. This gives you much more range with Misha to move the cows. I can teach you how to use it if you like."

"I heard they have whistles only dogs can hear," Jo said.

"Yep, but they are mostly used for hunting. Besides, who wants to blow into a whistle they can't hear? Doesn't sound like much fun."

Jo put the whistle to her lips and blew.

"Now you just have to figure out your list of commands and teach Misha what each sound means."

"This is going to be fun," smiled Jo.

She blew the whistle and Misha cocked her head at her.

"Like I said, she'll have to learn what each sound means," said Mr. Wills.

"Thanks, Mr. Wills. This is a swell gift."
"I thought you might like it."

CHAPTER 14

MISHA AND THE BEAR

Jo rode up the road atop Sundance in the newly fallen snow towards the old picnic area. Sundance was walking fast, his reins swinging with an even rhythm under his neck with each step he took.

Misha, as usual, was in a hurry up ahead. She stopped to smell a deer print on the trail. Looking with an attentive eye into the boughs of a pine tree, she heard what Jo thought was a talkative squirrel or a cackling blue jay.

Misha looked back at Sundance as if to say, "Hurry up, what is taking you so long?" Her eyes bright and ears up listening, Misha looked for anything that moved across her trail.

Suddenly Sundance stopped short, his body tightened and Jo sensed his nostrils were wide.

Jo took a deep breath.

Misha started to bark and move excitedly to and fro. Then Jo saw him, a large black bear lumbering through the pine trees and scrub oak ahead.

Jo held her horse's reins back to keep her distance, but Misha had more guts than a fox in a hen house. She ran toward the bear barking madly, stopping a few feet from him.

Misha lunged forward then just as quickly backed up. She did this over and over again, appearing to be dancing with the bear.

The bear seemed amused as he continued picking through the scrub for withered acorns and dried dead berries.

This game kept on until the bear, with one quick movement, fell on all four legs and ran toward Misha who up until now was the prima donna of the bear-dog ballet.

Misha held her ground long enough to see the bear was serious and the game was coming to a quick end. She ran back to Jo. Misha was shaking from head to toe.

The bear nonchalantly returned to eating and gave a look at the astonished girl, the horse and the dog that had never before known fear.

"Ah-ha! Check-mate! I win!" the bear seemed to say as it turned, shook its big rear end a few times and disappeared in the brush.

When the bear was safely far from sight Jo turned Sundance for home. Misha wagged her tail and trotted alongside them, looking up at Jo with a nervous smile.

"They're nothing like the cows," Jo scolded Misha. "Lucky the bear wasn't any hungrier or you'd be dog food."

Jo put her heels to Sundance and they trotted all the way home.

"That was a quick ride," said her mom when she arrived at the barn.

"We saw a bear on the trail."

"What did Misha do?" said her mom.

"Acted tough until the bear called her bluff."

Anne bent down and looked Misha in the eye. "I'll bet you're glad to be home safe and sound."

Misha licked her face over and over again.

"Don't let her fool you, mom. She was scared stiff."

Mrs. Wilson pet Misha up and down her back. "She's still shaking. Best get her inside and let her calm down by the fire. I'll put Sundance in the barn for you."

Jo slid off Sundance and walked towards the house, Misha at her side.

Mrs. Wilson took Sundance by the reins and led her to the barn, pausing to look up at the snow-covered hills to the west. She would have to have a family talk that night with her husband's help. A hungry bear in the dead of winter could have been disastrous for her only child and her brave little dog.

CHAPTER 15

THE BOX SUPPER

The parent-teacher conference at the school was held before President's Day. To enliven the evening conference and to encourage attendance by parents and their students it was better known as "The Box Supper." Parents were expected to bring dishes for a potluck dinner buffet.

The female students were encouraged to bring homemade desserts to the event to be sold off in a raffle to raise money for the school. The desserts had to be wrapped up and disguised. Only the men and boys were allowed to bid. Someone's dad always volunteered to be the auctioneer, offering each box to the highest bidder.

Many of the girls had taken classes in Home Economics and if they couldn't cook there was always a mother to pitch in and help them with a secret dessert recipe.

Jo had decided to bake a cherry pie after school. It surely smelled good coming out of the oven, she thought to herself. Now it was cooling.

Her stomach tightened at the thought of the evening. She went outside to take her mind off the whole idea.

Her mom yelled out the window. "Jo, help me pack the boxes for tonight." When Jo came back in the kitchen she found her mom admiring a decorated box on the table.

"I really like the way you decorated it."

Jo had spent the last four nights designing the box. She had painstakingly cut out silhouettes of presidents George Washington and Abraham Lincoln and painted cherry trees on the box with her set of watercolors. The box was lined inside with white butcher paper to make her cherry pie more appealing.

She had learned in school that Luke was an American history buff and she needed all the help she could get for him to notice her box and maybe buy it.

Jo closed the lid on her warm pie. Her mind wandered over the past months. Why did Luke tease her at recess? Why did he sit behind her in the classroom and pull her hair.

"Because he likes you," Hannah told her over and over again.

"So his bothering me is a good sign?"

"You bet," said Hannah. "I think he wants to be your boyfriend!"

"*Boyfriend*?" Jo shouted at her one day at recess. "He's the last boy on earth I'd want as a *boyfriend*."

"Sure, Jo. Whatever you say," Hannah winked. "We're best friends. It's our little secret."

Jo got so mad at Hannah she didn't talk to her all the way home on the bus that day.

Mrs. Wilson put her arms around Jo and kissed her on the cheek. "I just know tonight will be fun for you."

"Or completely dreadful," said Jo.

"Oh?" said her mom.

"There's a boy at school. You know him."

"Luke?"

"Yes. Luke. "

"He seems to be a nice boy. Todd certainly likes him."

"Todd wanted me to tell him how I was going to wrap my dessert box."

"What on earth for?"

"So he can tell Luke which one is mine."

"And?"

"So Luke can bid on it and win."

"Why, I think that is rather thoughtful," said her mom.

"I just don't understand boys," said Jo.

"Wait until they're older. It gets worse," laughed her mom. "When I was a senior in high school your father followed me around like a lame sick duck."

"How come?"

"Because he liked me."

"What did you do?"

"One day, I caught him on the school steps and confronted him."

"What did you say?"

"I said, 'Charlie Wilson, if you like me so much why don't you do something about it besides staring at me like you have a stomach ache all the time!'"

"You said that to dad?"

"Among other things."

Jo remained quiet for a spell, and then said, "There's a boy like that bothering Hannah. His name is Matt Turner. He kinda talks to her at the 4-H but at school he acts like somebody sewed his lips shut when he sees her."

Mrs. Wilson delicately filled one box with fried chicken and another with potato salad.

The phone rang and Anne talked to Aunt Claire for a few minutes before handing the phone over to Jo.

"It's Hannah," she said. "She wants to talk about tonight."

Jo rolled her eyes and picked up the receiver.

"Are you as excited as I am, Jo?" said Hannah.

"Maybe just a little," said Jo.

"What did you wrap your box with?"

"Silhouettes of presidents and cherry trees," said Jo. "You?"

"Fireworks," said Hannah.

"What dessert did you make?"

"Chocolate cake. And my mom baked a ham with pineapple sauce and coleslaw. What's your dessert?"

"Cherry pie, of course."

Jo's father came in from feeding the cattle.

"Better hurry and wash up," said Anne. "The Box Supper starts in thirty minutes."

"I'll be ready," said Charlie.

After he left the room Jo started laughing.

"What's so funny?" said her mother.

"I just pictured dad as a boy with a stomach ache."

Her mom giggled and wiggled Jo's ears. "Don't you say a word!"

"I won't," Jo promised.

Jo and her parents put on coats, hats, and gloves to brave the cold February night air.

Misha trotted up to Jo at the door and lowered her eyes.

"Sorry, Misha. I can't take you everywhere," Jo said.

Seven o'clock came. There was a buzz of activity. The accordion doors between the school rooms were slid open. Tables for eight were packed tightly together in the schoolhouse.

Pretty boxes filled with the fragrance of freshly-baked food were placed on the upright piano and side tables for all to see.

The secret dessert boxes were placed on a long table running the length of the chalkboard. The dads and their boys eyed each one, discussing among themselves who could have brought each box and what could be in them.

Jo caught Luke giving her a smile and a wink. She felt her face getting warm, hoping he'd go away. She backed up behind her dad.

Husbands and wives mingled for half an hour with teachers and friends talking about student grades and school improvements. The talk turned to cattle prices, new recipes, 4-H and sports.

In a loud voice the auctioneer interrupted the chatter. "Before we serve up supper, let's begin the bidding for the dessert boxes!"

The auction began. The men and boys moved closer as the bidding got started.

"Five dollars, ten dollars, sold!" the auctioneer said as a happy man walked away with a great smelling box.

Five more boxes were raised in the air, bid on and bought.

The auctioneer picked up a box decorated with red, white and blue fireworks.

"That's Hannah's," Jo whispered to her mom.

Hannah's box sold for ten dollars. Jo wasn't surprised at the winner.

"That's Matt," she whispered to her mom.

Five more boxes were bid on and sold.

Jo kept her eye on her box as the auctioneer held it up high for all to see. She saw Luke raise his arm up high and shout, "One dollar!"

The auctioneer pointed at another raised hand. "Five dollars!" shouted a man.

"Ten dollars!" said another.

Luke's hand was still up. The auctioneer missed him.

"Twelve dollars!" said Uncle John.

Jo glanced at Luke. He seemed to be counting a small wad of dollar bills in his hand.

"Going once, going twice..." said the auctioneer.

"Fifteen dollars!" shouted Luke.

"Going once, going twice," said the auctioneer.

"Sixteen dollars!" Luke shouted.

The auctioneer smiled at him. "You already bid fifteen dollars," he said. "You can't raise your own bid."

"Oh," Luke said sheepishly.

Jo smiled to herself. Poor Luke, she thought. He was so sweet.

"Going once again, now twice... sold to the boy with fifteen dollars!" said the auctioneer.

He handed Jo's box to Luke and took his fifteen dollars.

Proudly taking the box in his hands, Luke walked past Jo. "I can't eat this whole thing myself. Will you help me?"

"Sure," said Jo before she could think of saying 'no'.

After the auction the potluck supper was served up. When the meal was over, Luke visited Jo at her table. He was holding her cherry pie in his hands.

"Excuse me, Mr. and Mrs. Wilson," he said with a twinkle in his eye. "But I can't eat this whole pie by myself. Is it okay if Jo helps me eat it?"

Anne glanced at Jo. "What do you think, Jo?"

"Well," Jo said coyly. "Maybe a small piece." She pointed to an empty table near the back. "How about that one?" she managed to say.

By the time they reached the table, Hannah, Todd and Matt slid in next to them.

"I got chocolate cake," Matt bragged.

"I won a cherry pie," Luke bragged back. "I'll bet it tastes better."

"Why don't we all have a piece of each?" said Hannah as she passed out plates and forks.

Everyone agreed.

When the pie plate was empty and there was one piece of chocolate cake left, Luke declared Jo the winner.

"I'm not done yet!" complained Matt.

He picked up the last piece of cake and shoved it in his mouth. Halfway through, he reached for a carton of chocolate milk to wash it down.

"I think he's choking to death," said Todd.

"He's just a sore loser," said Luke.

Jo and Hannah exchanged secret glances, both delighted with the results of the evening.

"I sure wish I knew who baked that pie,"" added Luke. "I'd like to thank the chef personally."

"You know who baked that pie," Todd said. "Hannah already told you."

Jo's eyes narrowed at the betrayal.

Todd wasn't done letting the air out of his bag. "And don't you act so dumb either, Matt. I still got the quarter in my pocket from telling you which one was Hannah's."

Hannah stood and feigned her distaste. "Why, I never!" she said. "Come on, Jo!"

She marched away from the table with Jo close behind and they went to the back of the room.

Hannah broke into one of her famous big giggles.

"Why did we leave?" Jo asked.

"To make them suffer," Hannah said.

Hannah was smarter when it came to boys. After all, she was a whole year older than Jo.

As the evening came to an end, empty containers that once held food were put into the decorated boxes and lids were fastened. Hugs and smiles went around as coats, gloves and hats were put on.

On the drive home Jo thought about how nice it was to have good friends. She smiled even more thinking of Luke.

Going to the team roping in the spring with Hannah would be a lot of fun. After all, Luke would be there. He was Todd's partner.

CHAPTER 16

TEAM ROPING

Spring arrived. The snow melted off in most places on the foothills. The town of Colorado Springs had recently opened up an event center called Penrose Stadium to attract national rodeos, 4-H Clubs and a new national event called Little Britches Rodeo.

Todd and Luke would compete in their first ever calf team-roping event the last Saturday in April.

It was all the boys seemed to talk about at school in the weeks leading up to it. Todd put his ball cap aside and started wearing his cowboy hat to school every day to match Luke's.

When the big day came, Uncle John loaded up his trailer with Todd's horse Smokey.

"Can we take Misha?" Jo begged her parents.

"I don't see why not," said her dad. "We'll have to leave her in the truck when we watch Todd's event though. We'll bring a leash just in case."

Jo whistled for Misha to get in the back of the truck. The Wilsons followed the Marshall's rig to the new outdoor stadium.

There was a huge dirt parking lot with long rows of newly built wooden barns for boarded horses next to the stadium. Horse trailers of all sizes and shapes were parked everywhere with horses tied up to them.

Some boys were already adjusting blankets and saddles on their horses. Others were currying horses, picking loose pebbles from their hooves or combing their manes and tails. The horses sensed something was about to happen. Some were nickering, some were pawing the ground, others pacing.

Uncle John parked his rig as close as he could to the barns since he would have to carry water from the hand pumps built nearby. The Wilsons parked next to him.

As Todd unloaded Smokey, Luke arrived with his parents pulling a single horse trailer. Inside was Luke's horse Warrior. Warrior was an impressive bay quarter horse with a name that matched his looks.

Hannah took Jo by the sleeve and pulled her towards Luke as he unloaded Warrior. Jo felt butterflies in her stomach.

"We just wanted to wish you luck today," Hannah told Luke.

"Thanks," said Luke and he tipped his hat.

The girls went over to Todd and wished him luck next.

"It's all about our timing," Todd said rather maturely. "If the dirt is right and the calf runs straight we should be okay."

Smokey was prancing, ears up and snorting, as Todd got a tight grip, one hand close to the bit, the other hand holding the rest of the reins. He tightened the cinches, adjusted the headstall and backed Smokey away from the trailer to calm him down.

Misha came up to Smokey and stood in front of him. She lowered her head and stared up at the horse. It seemed to calm Smokey down.

Finally the boys saddled and watered their horses and led them to a long fence. They grabbed their rope lariats and found a fence post nearby to practice their throws. They were strictly business.

"Will you look at Todd?" Charlie Wilson said. "I swear he looks ten years older right now."

"And three inches taller since last year," said his wife.

Aunt Claire gave Charlie some tickets. "We'll find you in the seats," she said.

After they put Misha in the truck, Charlie and Anne led the girls to the arena entrance. A few retail booths had been set up in in the walkways of the arena outside the seating area.

Everyone stopped at a booth that sold hot chocolate. It wasn't as good as Anne's homemade hot chocolate but it took the edge off the morning chill.

The Wilsons and Hannah took their front row seats. Jo looked at the rectangular arena.

"It's so big!" she said.

"Team-roping requires a standard area of 120 feet wide by 150 feet long," said her dad. He pointed to the left. "See that narrow chute with the closed gate? There's a man there next to a buzzer. When the gate swings open the time clock starts ticking."

They heard an announcer's voice: "Team roping starts in fifteen minutes."

Jo glanced at the calves used for the event. "They're so big!" she said.

"They're two year olds," said her father, "Todd and Luke will have their hands full."

Uncle John and Aunt Claire arrived and took their seats.

"What are the rules again?" Anne asked Uncle John.

Uncle John explained, "One roper is the header. He throws his lariat first with a large loop over the head of the calf. Once the calf is caught he pulls the calf to the left and dallies his rope around the saddle horn, tying it with a few short light loops. This keeps the rope tight and helps the horse hold the calf. Then the heeler works his magic by roping both hind feet. The heeler dallies his rope around the saddle horn, then header and heeler face each other and back their horses up until there is no slack on the ropes. That's when the buzzer stops and their time is recorded. It takes amazing coordination and cooperation for the riders and their horses."

"First draw is Tommy Parker and Billy Sutters," said the announcer.

The crowd took a collective breath as two young cowboys rode into the arena and took their places. The first boy roper in the arena was the header. He rode a few dozen feet and pulled his horse to a stop. The header swung his lariat over his head, gaining top speed and a full loop as his other hand held the rest of the loose length of lariat rope in his other hand for the toss that was supposed to land around the calf's neck.

The second roper, the heeler, entered the arena and took up a position close to the gate where the calf was supposed to run out. Like the header, he worked his lariat above his head, waiting for the gate to fly open and the calf to come running out of the chute.

The buzzer sounded and the gate swung open. A big calf ran into the arena and the young cowboys galloped after it. The header missed his toss and the calf trotted off across the arena.

"No score," said the announcer.

"They missed their catch," said John.

"Does that mean they are eliminated?" said Jo.

"Each team gets three tries," said Uncle John. "Each score is added together for their final overall score."

Three more pairs of young ropers tried their best. The second team's header snagged his calf but the heeler missed his loop on the calf's heels.

The third team's calf came out of the chute, stopped and turned right and trotted away from the line of action.

"I didn't think it was so hard," said Jo.

"Team-roping is the most technical event in rodeo," said her dad.

The announcer spoke: "Next up we have Todd Wilson and Luke Ford. Good luck, cowboys."

Todd rode into the arena as the header. Luke took his position as heeler. The boys nodded to each other with an air of confidence as if to say "ready," waiting for the buzzer as they swung their lariats in perfect precision over their heads.

The buzzer sounded. The gate flew open. Todd and Luke sprung their horses into action at a gallop.

But there was no calf to chase.

"False start," said the announcer. "Let's try it again with some beef in the chute this time."

Most of the crowd seemed to be standing, staring at the chute to see if there really was a calf being led in.

Todd and Luke rode back to their original positions, rewound their lariats and prepared for the next attempt. They nodded to each other again as their lariats swung above their heads.

Everyone could see a big calf in the chute now. This was the real deal.

The buzzer sounded. The gate flew open and the calf came darting out.

Just as it passed Todd, he tossed his lariat over its neck, fed the rope a little and followed the secured running calf, giving Luke time to make his throw.

Luke came right up behind the running calf and tossed a nice hard loop under its hind legs. He pulled on the lariat to cinch the knot.

Both boys worked furiously at either end of the calf, wrapping their remaining loose ropes on their saddle horns until the calf's rear legs lifted off the ground. Todd turned Smokey to face Luke and Warrior and the buzzer sounded.

The Wilsons and Marshalls jumped up in their seats, clapping and whistling.

"Did you see that?" yelled Uncle John to the people around him. That's my boy!"

Other pairs roped. Some scored and a few missed.

Todd and Luke roped again. Todd snagged the calf's head with his rope but the calf turned sideways on him and Luke missed his toss.

On their third ride out of the chute, Todd circled a nice loop over his head, extended his arm as far as he could and let the loop fly over the calf's neck. At the back of the calf Luke opened his rope wide and low with a loop that caught both hind legs. The boys dallied fast on the saddle horns and both horses pulled their ropes taut. The buzzer sounded and the ropers received their second good score.

Loud claps and whistles were heard all around the arena when the announcer gave the final scores. Todd Marshall and Luke Ford had won the first team-roping event of their lives.

Back at the trailers, Todd and Luke kicked at the dirt as parents and friends fawned over them.

"We had a good feelin' about it goin' in," Todd said without bragging.

Jo noticed that Todd's voice was changing. It was deeper than before. He was also dropping off the letter "g" at the end of his words. Just like a real cowboy, she supposed.

"Isn't roping fun?" Hannah asked Jo as they let Misha out of the truck for a walk.

"It is fun!" said Jo.

"Let's walk up and down the row of barns," said Hannah. "I'll bet there are some jumpers in the stalls."

Jo followed after Hannah with Misha by her side.

"So now Todd is roping and I'm going to start training Lily to jump. What about you and Misha?" said Hannah.

"What do you mean?"

"When you got her from Mr. Wills you said she would be the best herding dog ever. Is she?"

"She will be by the end of summer," said Jo.

"Promise?"

Jo bit her lip and looked at Misha. "What do you think, girl? You ready to go to work?"

Misha barked three times.

"I'll take that as a 'yes.'"

CHAPTER 17

SECOND SUMMER

Weeks before school ended Hannah was placing her saddle on Lily to get her used to its feel. Hannah's voice commands and the use of a headstall were commonplace to Lily now. Hannah would lead her on walks in the pastures or sometimes ride April, leading Lily behind or at her side. Lily was responding well to the ground work.

Hannah thought it was finally time to climb into the saddle and "test the waters."

She needed her dad's permission.

"Dad, Lily is doing really well in the exercise pen and on our walks in the hills and pastures with April. I was wondering... Do you think I can start riding her? I know I can't ride her long or hard because her legs are still developing but I thought I could start to ride her a few minutes a day in the exercise pen these next few months. Then maybe by summer's end she'll be ready to ride to Pikeview with me and Jo when we pay our ice cream tab."

"Let me watch the two of you in the exercise pen for a time with the ground work and we'll go from there," her dad said with a smile in his voice.

"And then she'll have to learn to jump," said Hannah.

"Of course," said her dad. "You don't think I bought you that fancy saddle for decoration, did you?"

Hannah smiled and rode April over to Jo's to tell her the great news.

Jo was in one of the pastures with Misha. She was holding the whistle Mr. Wills had given her.

"You know how to use it yet?" Hannah asked.

"Not really," said Jo.

"How many commands are there?"

"Six, I think. Misha knows my voice commands but sometimes when I blow the whistle she gets confused. She's good with two whistles so far. Let me show you."

Jo had been taking Misha out among the cows and calves all year. Now that it was summer, the grass was up in the fields and the cows and calves were grazing quietly.

Jo, Hannah and Misha moved to one side of the herd to get behind them.

Misha sensed her time was coming. She waited for Jo's whistle signal.

Jo took a good look at the herd. She made several short clicking sounds with her tongue and blew a low note on the whistle.

Misha sprang into action. She crouched in a low position and walked slowly towards the herd from behind.

Jo said loudly, "Way up, Misha, way up." She blew a higher pitch on the whistle.

Misha picked out a straggling cow and made eye contact known as "giving the eye."

The cow stared back at her. It was a matter of wills between the cow and Misha who was going to move first.

The straggler pawed at the ground and lowered her head.

Misha took slow small steps towards it. She didn't make a sound.

"What are they doing?" Hannah asked.

"Facing off. If the cow turns and moves towards the herd, Misha wins."

Misha barked once.

The cow shook its head, turned and ran to catch up with the rest of the herd.

"Misha wins again!" Jo smiled.

Jo blew her whistle three times. A low note, a medium note and a high note.

Misha ran back and forth behind the herd, sweeping them together in a cluster before they moved together, their sides nearly touching in the direction of the barn. If a cow or calf fell out of the herd Misha ran towards them and barked. The docile animals would fall back in the herd and keep moving in Misha's intended direction.

Jo jogged behind Misha with Hannah hurrying to catch up.

"That was impressive!" said Hannah.

"Maybe for you. I blew the wrong notes. Misha was supposed to come back to me and sit. Let me try this again." Jo called out, "Way up, Misha, way up." Jo raised her arm in the air above her head and made a large circling motion. "Circle, Misha. Circle."

Misha slowed her pace and began to trot around the herd, getting them in a tighter and tighter circle until the herd was standing head to tail and came to a full stop. Misha walked around the circled cows and calves. The herd stood motionless.

Jo said, "Good dog."

"That is amazing!" said Hannah.

Misha lay down on the ground, her eyes to the herd for any movement. If a cow or calf started to wander Misha was there to make sure they stayed in the circle with a short bark or nip at the heels.

"I'd say you've been practicing," Hannah said as Misha steered the herd towards the barn again.

"Misha has my hand signals down pat," Jo said. She looked at the whistle in her hand. "Darned whistle. It seems simple but it's like learning to play a violin! So frustrating!"

They returned to the barn. Jo's dad was there, pouring feed in the troughs.

"How did Misha do today?" he asked.

"Count the cows and see for yourself," Jo said proudly. She climbed up on a fence rail. "So dad, I've been thinking maybe it's time for a contest for Misha. What about Steamboat Springs?"

"Steamboat Springs? That is one of the best contests in the West. Are you sure you want that one for Misha's first?" He eyed Jo with a look of wonder in his eyes.

"May as well start at the top."

"What do you think?" Charlie asked Hannah.

Hannah thought for a moment. "I want to take Lily to the Grand National someday. I don't know that we'll ever get that far. Steamboat Springs is just a day away. Besides, Misha is pretty amazing."

"Okay then. Steamboat Springs it is," said Mr. Wilson.

"You watch, dad. Misha is the best cow dog ever. You'll see."

"I believe you, Jo."

"Do you think Mr. Wills can help? I'm having trouble with my whistle."

"I'm sure he won't mind."

CHAPTER 18

LILY JUMPS

It had been almost a year since that rainy afternoon when Lily was born. Lily and Hannah were receiving great training from Miss McClure, a professional jumping trainer. She worked at the best horse training school in Colorado Springs.

"Lily sure loves to jump," Hannah told Miss McClure when they finished the jump course at the large indoor arena. Hannah was dressed in an English riding outfit.

"I think Lily is ready for a little more of a challenge," stated Miss McClure.

"She is?"

"So are you. Lily has good leg extensions over the jumps. She has good eyes. Knows her heights and what it takes to clear. Let's put her in her first competition next Saturday."

Hannah exhaled slowly. She patted Lily on the neck and said, "Okay."

Jo walked up from the fence rail. "It's what you always dreamed of."

"I know," said Hannah. "It seems like yesterday when Lily was born."

The following Saturday came too soon for Hannah.

"What's wrong?" asked Jo as they arrived at the arena with their families.

"Maybe Lily is ready, but I'm not so sure about me," admitted Hannah.

"After the first jump you'll be fine," said Jo.

"What makes you so sure?"

"It's the start of your dream."

Before the start of the event Hannah walked Lily around with a lead rope attached to her halter to limber her up.

"I sure wish you could talk, Lily. You know talking always helps with the butterflies in the stomach," said Hannah.

Hannah tied Lily to the side of the trailer when they returned. She picked up Lily's legs one at a time and cleaned out the dirt and pebbles wedged in her shoes. Brushing Lily,

Hannah thought back over the past months of training and said to herself, "Yes we are ready."

She wrapped Lily's legs tightly with leg wraps for support, put the saddle on, tightened the girth and got on.

"Let's show them what we got," she told Lily as they rode to the arena entrance. A group of people was waving to her from the stands. Hannah thought she saw Jo and her family and waved back. She was terrified.

Miss McClure was waiting for her at the starting gate. "The jumps will be a little higher and wider, not much of a difference from what you're used to, but enough that Lily will sense it and you will feel her extend her legs more upward as she goes over the jump. Relax the reins and let Lily lead. Trust her and remember... she was born to jump."

Hannah nodded and adjusted her riding helmet. She eyed the jumping obstacles in the arena. "They don't look that different," she decided.

An official with a clipboard walked up to her. "You're next," he said. "Wait about a minute until the jumper ahead of you clears the arena. Go when you're ready."

"Is there a buzzer?" Hannah asked.

"No. No buzzer," smiled the official. "This is a refined sport. Take it nice and easy. You'll both be fine."

Hannah waited for the last jumper to clear the arena. She relaxed in her saddle, eased up on the reins, gave Lily a gentle tap with her boot heel and took a deep breath. Lily knew what to do. She galloped with an easy long stride towards the first jump, pacing herself. She cleared the first jump like a pro.

Hannah exhaled and said, “Lily you are an amazing horse,” as they rode on towards the next hurdle.

The two continued the jumping course with only one mishap. Lily’s left hind leg tapped the top rail on a jump as she cleared it. The rail fell off and rolled to the ground. It sounded like thunder to Hannah. It was much different than a rodeo. She didn’t expect such a quiet and refined audience. The loudest sounds from the stands seemed to be whispers.

When Hannah and Lily cleared the last hurdle Miss McClure was waiting for them at the finish.

“You and Lily did great!” Miss McClure said.

Hannah got off and gave Lily a big hug. Miss McClure guided them back to their trailer.

The Marshalls and Wilsons ran down from the stands and congratulated Hannah.

“How did the saddle feel?” her dad asked.

“Were you nervous?” said Todd. “You looked nervous.”

“Lily flew through the air!” said Hannah’s mom.

“You were great!” said her uncle Charlie.

“You two were wonderful,” said her aunt Anne.

Hannah unsaddled Lily. She laid the saddle on the ground and unwound the leg wraps, placing them in the box that held all the important things for horse care; Aloe-heal, combs, shampoo and hoof picks. Lily munched on some hay while Hannah brushed her.

Hannah realized Jo was missing. “Where did she vanish to?” Hannah wondered.

Hannah took Lily by the lead and thanked everyone for coming. “I’m going to walk Lily for a few minutes to cool her off before we head home,” she said.

As she walked Lily she saw Jo coming towards her carrying two ice cream cones.

“Congratulations!” Jo shouted. “You were awesome!”

Hannah looked at the cones. “What is this?” she said.

"A little reward for a job well done."

Hannah studied the cones again. "They're both chocolate," she said. "You only eat vanilla."

"Am I allowed to change just a little?" Jo smiled.

The girls found a bench and sat down. Lily hovered over them, wondering if there might be a bite left for her.

Hannah and Jo sat in silence, watching people pass by. Finally, Hannah said, "So much has happened between us, Jo. Remember what we promised each other? That our friendship will last to the moon and back, and then some?"

"I remember," said Jo.

"I wish I could wake up tomorrow and never get old again," Hannah sighed.

"You know that's not going to happen," said Jo.

"I know. But we can wish, can't we?"

"Always."

When Hannah and Jo returned to the trailer with Lily, Miss McClure was showing Claire Marshall pamphlets of a new riding school up in Denver called The Horse Park.

"Hannah has shared her wish of riding in the Grand National in England with me," Miss McClure said.

"I'm not surprised," said her mom. "She has high and lofty dreams. Dreams are good. We don't discourage her."

"I think she and Lily can go all the way," added Miss McClure. "This is the best school in the state. On the expensive side, but they produce winners."

Claire took the pamphlets and put them in her purse. "We'll take a look," she said. "We want what is best for Hannah."

"And that's The Horse Park!"

"We'll have to discuss this with Hannah," Claire said.

"Of course. Whatever is best for Hannah." Miss McClure smiled and started walking away.

"Thanks for your help today," Hannah called after Miss McClure.

Her instructor turned back towards her, nodded and kept on walking.

"You and Lily were wonderful," Claire said to Hannah.

"Lily was wonderful," said Hannah. "I just held on."

Her mom gave her a weak smile. There were small tears in her eyes.

"What is it mom? What's wrong?"

"Oh, I just hate to see you growing up so quickly. I'll wake up one day and poof! You'll be gone."

"Come on, mom! We have lots of time to spend together. I'm not even a teenager yet."

CHAPTER 19

LEARNING THE WHISTLE

That spring Jo didn't see Hannah or Todd nearly as much as she used to.

Hannah was busy with Lily taking jumping lessons.

Todd was practicing with Luke for their next team-roping event or tending to his small flock of young turkeys, lining up customers to sell them to when the turkeys were old enough. Todd made sure not to name any of the turkeys and kept them in a large confined area except for Tom who still enjoyed his usual freedoms.

Jo practiced in the pastures with Misha and her whistle.

Mr. Wills stopped by for an hour at least once a week to watch their progress with the cows and calves. One day on the Wilson porch after a training break he and Jo shared a heart-to-heart talk. Anne Wilson had provided them with a pitcher of fresh lemonade and cookies.

"You're getting better with the whistle every day," said Mr. Wills as he ate a cookie. "But there's more to it than just blowing out sound. You need to practice on pitch and tone more. They mean something to Misha too."

"That makes sense," Jo said.

"A whistle is better than words. Words flow. A whistle is consistent. It isn't personal. A dog learns what the tone in your voice means. How many ways are there to say 'sit'?"

"It depends on what mood I'm in or what mischief Misha is in."

"Exactly."

"And sometimes when I say 'Misha come,' I say it in a gentle fun tone and she comes with her tail wagging or if I say it in a stern tone she comes with her tail between her legs and her head down."

Mr. Wills took another cookie from the plate. "Now a whistle, it means the same thing every time."

"Like a tiger is a tiger." Jo said with a laugh.

"Yes, you got it." Mr. Wills smiled. "I like that... a tiger is a tiger. I'm going to remember that. A whistle is just a command. It doesn't mean a good job or a bad job. It just asks Misha to do something. Let me see that whistle."

Jo had it tied to a string around her neck. She pulled it off and handed it to Mr. Wills. He bounced the whistle up and down in his hand.

"When you blow into the whistle start by placing your tongue on the top of the back seam. Here. Try making a squeak."

He handed her back the whistle. Jo tried and tried but no squeak.

"Looks like you're tongue-tied," said Mr. Wills. "Give me that whistle again."

Jo handed him the whistle.

"Watch my tongue," he said. He opened his mouth wide and held the whistle up to it. "Thee?" he said.

Jo laughed.

Mr. Wills pulled the whistle out. "See how my tongue was bent?" He handed her back the whistle. "Try again."

Jo inserted the whistle, bent her tongue and blew a high squeaking noise after many tries.

"Oops," she smiled. "I think I just swallowed a mouse."

"No, that was good!" said Mr. Wills. "A new sound for you. Now I want you to practice that squeak by making different tones like a flute player."

"Like a flute player?"

"Like a Pied Piper! You only use five or six tones to herd cattle."

"Whew," Jo said with relief. "You had me scared for a little bit. I thought there might be more."

"Heck, I tried singing to my cows one year," Mr. Wills said. "It didn't turn out well."

"What happened?"

"The cows ran away."

"Did you ever get them back?"

"Sure, after they made me sign a letter promising I would never sing to them again."

Jo laughed and laughed.

"I want you to practice that whistle while you walk around the barn and back. Go on!" he prompted.

Jo adjusted her ball cap and hiked off towards the barn blowing into the whistle. Her squeaks made different tones but they were still squeaks.

Mr. Wills found a chair under a tree in the front yard and sat with Misha at his side. Misha's ears didn't know what to make of Jo's music yet.

"It will come to you, Misha. Just you wait," he said as he rubbed her behind the ears.

When Jo returned she sat in the grass next to Misha.

"Now I want you to practice every day, everywhere you can but not around Misha," he said. "We don't want to wreck her."

"Okay, Mr. Wills."

He returned a week later and was amazed by Jo's progress. She had learned six tones. They were clear and concise.

"I thought my tongue was gonna fall off but I finally got them!" Jo smiled.

"Good job, Jo," he said. "Now let's assign your herding words. One for each tone," he said.

"Great!"

They put Misha in the barn and walked far away from the house so Misha couldn't hear them and Mr. Wills began his next round of lessons.

"It will take about a day for Misha to understand what each whistle's tone means," said Mr. Wills. "Let's practice with the first whistle. We'll have to run the same exercise over and over again until you and Misha are sick of it. Ready?"

"Ready."

They returned to the barn. Jo called to Misha. "Come on, girl. We have work to do!"

"Okay," said Mr. Wills. "Let's find us some cows and their calves to play with."

CHAPTER 20

COUNTING THE HERD

At the end of spring the baby calves smelled the flowers and enjoyed their momma's milk. It was time for the Spring Round Up.

Charlie Wilson needed his head count so he could call the vet to vaccinate them for different diseases. He always made sure to take care of every animal.

Misha circled around the pasture collecting baby calves. She looked under the wild plum bushes. She looked in the scrub oaks. She looked next to the big apple tree. She shook the cows and calves from their lazy ways and the herd responded. Misha was born to her responsibilities and Jo took great pride in the fact that she had chosen her.

Misha barked and nipped at the heels of the mommas and their babies and moved them towards the barn. She truly enjoyed sweeping the pasture behind the herd as it stubbornly moved in step to her commands.

Clipboard in hand, Charlie Wilson opened the corral gate and watched as cow after cow marched in, complacent and obedient to Misha's commands. The calves were in tow, fearful from straying.

"Good girl!" Charlie said. Jo noticed that her father patted Misha a lot behind the ears or on her hindquarters. "She sure makes things easier," he said. "Day by day Misha is honing her skills."

Jo held up her whistle. “We’re starting to figure things out.”

Some afternoons, when Hannah wasn’t up north learning to be a jumper with Lily, Jo rode to Pikeview with her for ice cream.

“You’re back to vanilla, I see,” Hannah joked. “What happened to chocolate?”

“I’m saving chocolate for special occasions,” Jo said.

Mrs. Reed was still at the store, still wearing the same gingham dress. The girls wondered if they would recognize her wearing anything else.

CHAPTER 21

APRIL DIES

John Marshall had been working in the pasture. He noticed April wasn't with the other horses. He pulled his ball cap down to block the sun in his eyes. Squinting, he turned in a small circle looking for her. As he looked into the trees by the stream he noticed her body on the ground.

"Oh no," he said to himself and ran to her.

April was lying on her side struggling to get up. John instinctively started to push her back and forth, rocking her to help her get up. She was just too heavy.

"April, I am going for help. Lay still, girl."

He ran back to the barn and saw Todd raking manure into a wheelbarrow in one of the corrals.

"Todd! April is down and I can't get her up. Get your mother and sister!"

Todd ran inside the barn and returned with Hannah and their mother.

"What's wrong with April?" said Hannah.

"Colic maybe. Hannah, grab April's halter and lead," John ordered. "Todd, open the pasture gate. When I drive through, close it behind us."

He ran to his truck and started it.

Hannah returned from the barn with the halter and lead and jumped in the truck with her parents. They drove through the gate and waited for Todd to close it behind them and join them in the truck.

As John drove he spoke rapidly. "It will take the four of us to get April on her feet," he said.

"Then what?" said Hannah.

"I'm not sure."

He pulled the truck up near April. The family ran up to her.

"Easy, girl," John said as he put his ear to April's stomach. After a short spell he looked at his family. "No sounds. Hannah, get that halter on her. We need to stand her up."

Hannah was already at April's head. She slipped the halter on her head and snapped the lead to the ring on the halter. John, Claire and Todd got beside April and started rocking her back and forth, pushing on her back, hoping she would put her front feet out and get up.

Hannah tugged on the halter and lead. "Come on, April! Please get up! Please!"

"What's colic?" Todd asked his parents.

Claire explained as they continued rocking April. "It's how horses eat," she said. "If they eat too fast, they don't digest their food. It's very painful. That's why April laid down. Usually the intestine gets twisted and causes constipation. A bowel movement is always a welcome sign."

"Okay everyone, one more good push!" John yelled.

April shook her head, put her front legs out and stood up.

"Walk her back to the barn," said John. "Don't let her stop. She'll want to lay down again but you can't let her."

Hannah started walking her.

John looked to Claire and Todd. "Stay with them. Don't let April lay down! I'll call Doc Brown!"

Hannah started shaking as she led April. Calling the family veterinarian was never a good sign. By the time she reached the barn with her mother and brother her father was there, passing out jackets as the sun dipped over the mountains to the west.

"Doc Brown is on his way," he said. "Thirty minutes out." He slipped a jacket over Hannah's shoulders. "Keep her moving."

Hannah walked April in circles in the corral next to the barn. As the dusk crept in, she felt a surreal moment looking at the sparse grass of summer taking hold, seeing the buds on the aspen and scrub oak trees. A lone pine tree in the distance stood like a sentinel in the cool of approaching darkness. She felt the wind pick up on her face.

Todd walked up to her and offered to walk April. He knew Hannah wouldn't give up the lead but he wanted to show his support.

"No thanks," said Hannah. "Can you call Jo for me? I really need her."

"Okay," said Todd. He jumped a fence and ran towards the house. As his parents passed him in the yard, he shouted, "Hannah wants me to call Jo."

"Ask your uncle Charlie and Aunt Anne to come too," said John. "We may need them."

Todd called the Wilsons. They were on their way. He brought a glass of water out to Hannah and a bucket of water for April. Hannah and April refused to drink.

"Let's get April to the barn," said John. "I see headlights."

The Marshalls led April towards the barn just as Doc Brown and the Wilsons arrived. Doc Brown climbed out of his truck with a big black bag. Charlie Wilson had his doctor's bag just in case.

"Looks like colic," said John nervously. "I couldn't hear anything in her stomach."

Doc Brown studied April as she walked. "Her head's down. Sluggish footsteps," he said. "I think you're right. Let's get her inside."

Everyone walked with April into the barn. Doc Brown pulled a stethoscope from his bag and listened to her heart. "She's beating fast," he said. He listened to her stomach next. "Nothing," he said.

Hannah and Jo held hands and said a silent prayer.

"I need a bucket of warm water," said the vet as he pulled a long hollow tube from his bag.

Everyone waited as Claire and Anne ran to the house. They returned with a large bucket of warm water from the kitchen sink.

"It's nice and warm," said Claire.

"Let's tube her," said Doc Brown.

"Do what? Hannah asked. She had never seen a horse this sick and she didn't know what the vet was about to do. She squeezed Jo's hand.

"I'll explain as I go," said Doc Brown. "First I am going to give April a shot in her neck to make her relax." He raised a large horse syringe, tapped it to get the air out, found a vein on April's neck and plunged the needle in.

April flinched a little. Soon she was swaying on her legs, her head down and eyes closed.

Doc Brown grabbed the bucket of warm water and submerged the open tube into it. He took the other end in his mouth and sucked on it until water ran out.

"Now the hard part," he said. "We need to get to her organs with the liquid." He stuck a pair of fingers up one of April's nostrils and inserted the hose. Some of the water spilled out and dripped on the floor of the barn.

Hannah grimaced. "You're hurting her!"

"She doesn't feel a thing from the shot I just gave her," said Doc Brown. "April is fine. She knows we're trying to help her."

Soon the bucket was empty. Doc Brown withdrew the tube from April's nostril.

April was still swaying. Everyone stood around her to keep her standing.

"Once the tranquilizer wears off, you'll need to keep walking her," said Doc Brown. "What she needs is a good bowel movement. A nice pile of manure would be a welcome sight." He gathered up his instruments and stuffed them in his black bag. "Not much else we can do for now but wait."

The adults took a short break for a cup of coffee with the doctor at the house. It would take twenty minutes for the tranquilizer to wear off before Hannah could exercise April in the corral.

It was black outside without the help of a moon hidden in the clouds when Hannah led April to the corral. Jo was with her for every step.

"This is what best friends are for," she told Hannah.

They didn't get far when April's knees started to buckle.

"Help!" Hannah screamed.

Todd ran up to the house and fetched the adults. They came running. By the time they got there April was down. They tried and tried to get her up but to no avail.

Uncle John shook his head, swearing under his breath. There were tears in his eyes. "I can't take this. I can't see her suffer."

John pulled Doc Brown aside to speak privately.

Hannah sat down next to April and lifted her head in her lap, patting her and talking to her in soothing tones. April's breathing was irregular. Tears ran down Hannah's cheeks. Jo sat down next to her and cried with her.

Hannah shared her memories of rides in the hills and to Pikeview. Claire shared the story of when April was born.

Doc Brown retrieved his bag and approached April.

"No, dad! No!" Hannah cried.

Her dad's voice was tired. "It's time, Hannah. April is in a lot of pain. She can't open her eyes."

No one spoke as Doc Brown prepared a large needle. "She was a wonderful animal," he said."

"You can't!" said Hannah. "She'll get up any minute. You'll see."

Doc Brown knelt beside her. "She's suffering, Hannah. Can't you see? You have to say goodbye to her. You love her, don't you?"

"Yes."

"Then let her go."

Hannah tucked her head against April's, tears streaming as she finally whispered in April's ear and said goodbye. She stood up and wrapped herself around Todd.

Doc Brown knelt down, patted April gently on the neck and injected the needle.

Her body relaxed for the last time.

John Marshall removed the halter from April's head as Claire and Ann led the girls to the house. He bent over, cut a swath of hair from April's tail and tucked it in his pocket.

"For Hannah," he told Todd. "When she's ready."

"What do we do with April?" asked Todd.

His father found a tarp and covered April. "We'll bury her tomorrow in the wild plums. Hannah will like that."

CHAPTER 22

STEAMBOAT WHISTLE

The fall colors of late September were striking against the backdrop of mountains covered with pine trees. Higher up an early snow had left the mountain peaks white. The aspen trees had just started to turn their magnificent golden hues, their leaves dancing in the wind like small butterflies.

Steamboat Springs sat in a high mountain valley, a six hour drive north from the Wilson Ranch. It was already dark when Charlie Wilson pulled off the highway on the outskirts of the small town.

"There's the local feed lot," he said, pointing at hundreds of cows in a big pen. He pointed again. "Over there is the pasture, corral and pens for tomorrow's contest."

He drove up to the pens and stopped the truck.

"Have a look, Jo. Those are your competition cows."

Several cows approached the fence and mooed at them.

"And hello to you," laughed Jo.

Misha was excited. Her ears were up, eyes moving to and fro as she saw the cows. She climbed over Jo and barked out the open window.

Jo laughed and patted her on the head. "Misha says hello, too," Jo called out to the cows.

"Now that we have all met, can we please drive to the motel?" said Claire. "It's over on Main Street."

Charlie put the truck in gear and drove on.

"See you tomorrow," Jo shouted out her window at the cows.

When they pulled up to the motel Grandpa Henry and Grandma Elizabeth waved to them from the balcony outside their room.

Jo waved to them as she jumped out of the truck. “Thanks for coming!”

“We wouldn’t have missed it!” said her grandma.

The Wilsons went to the office to check in. The Marshalls met them in the lobby and helped them carry their luggage to their room.

“Can Hannah and I take Misha for a walk?” Jo begged. “It was a long ride.”

“Don’t get lost,” said her mother.

It was cold outside. The girls pulled down their ball caps and hurried to the parking lot with Misha.

Todd ran after them. “Hey, I’m coming too.”

The kids walked down the sidewalk on Main Street behind Misha. All the stores were closed for the night. Misha stopped and smelled the sidewalk, parking meters, doorways, and planted trees.

“Look!” said Hannah. “They have a JC Penney just like home.”

“And a hardware store,” Todd pointed out.

When they returned to the motel they went to their grandparents’ room and had sandwiches with the adults.

“How many competitors tomorrow?” Grandpa Henry asked Jo.

“Just ten,” said Jo. “Misha and I represent El Paso County.”

“That’s quite an honor.”

Anne added, “Jo and Misha were the best in 4-H this summer. All the local ranchers gave her their vote of support.”

“Welcome to the big time! Whatever happens tomorrow, you should always be proud you got this far,” Grandpa Henry told Jo.

“Time for bed everybody,” announced Grandma Elizabeth. “Jo and Misha have a big day tomorrow.”

Back in her room, Jo had a full size bed just for her and Misha.

“I’m glad we came up early so we can get used to the altitude,” said Anne.

"I didn't notice," said Jo with a yawn.

Misha did. She jumped up on the foot of the bed and fell asleep with Jo.

"Those two," Anne smiled. "They're inseparable."

In the morning Jo fed Misha before the kids led the adults back to Main Street in search of a breakfast café. There was a chill in the air.

"We saw two places last night," said Hannah.

"Do they say 'EATS'?" Grandma Elizabeth said.

"No," said Hannah.

"Good. I don't like restaurants named 'EATS'. The food is always terrible."

They stopped outside a restaurant named "Cowboy Café."

"Looks okay by me," said Grandpa Henry as he smelled the aroma of coffee coming from the door.

Grandma Elizabeth put her hands on her hips, deciding. Finally she said, "This will do. Let's eat."

The waitress was friendly. "Are you here for the herding competition?"

"Yes," said Charlie. "My daughter's in it."

Jo tipped her ball cap to the waitress.

"Let's get her fed then. She'll need her energy," said the waitress. She tapped Jo on her ball cap. "Family style okay? Oatmeal, scrambled eggs, bacon and sausage. We serve our French toast with real maple syrup. Coffee for the adults? Hot chocolate for the kids? Orange juice all around?"

Everyone agreed.

The food flew out of the kitchen and the waitress was never far away with refills from a stainless steel coffee pot. She also put whipped cream on top of the hot chocolates.

Todd showed off his white mustache. "Think I should start shaving?" he asked Grandma Elizabeth.

When Charlie finished his fifth cup of coffee he reached for the check.

Grandpa Henry intercepted it. “This one’s on me.” He paid the bill with a big tip.

Charlie stood and pulled on his coat. “You ready for the competition?” he asked Jo.

“Yep,” said Jo as she swallowed the bottom of her hot chocolate.

“Saddle up everybody!” Uncle John said.

The families hurried back to the motel. While the men started their engines the women retrieved Misha from her room after a good brushing.

They arrived at the fairgrounds in five minutes with plenty of time for Jo and Misha to get the jitters out while her parents signed her in with the competition officials.

Hannah and Todd tagged along with Jo and Misha. They passed barking dogs and their anxious owners. Misha trotted along. She seemed to be studying the competition.

When they reached the large pen that held the competition cows, Jo and Misha stood by the metal rail and watched them in silence. Some of the cows made eye contact with Misha and she stared right back at them, letting them know she was in charge.

“I never saw Misha so intense,” said Hannah.

“She’s looking for the queen, the leader. In every herd there’s always one stubborn cow that thinks she’s in charge. If we pull that cow in the draw, Misha will have her work cut out for her.”

Misha cocked her ears. There was a cow across the pen staring back at her.

“Misha found the leader,” said Jo. “See the cow with the big patch of white around her eye? Watch what happens.”

The cow lowered its head.

Misha raised hers.

The white-eyed cow slowly crossed the pen towards Misha, other cows moving aside for the queen.

Misha didn’t move. Her eyes were locked on the cow.

The cow came up to the guard rail and lowered its head even further. She was eye to eye with Misha.

“Wait for it!” said Jo.

"Wait for what?" said Hannah.

"Whoever moves first loses."

The stare-down continued until at last the cow blinked, turned its head and trotted back to the herd.

"Misha won! She beat White Eye!" smiled Jo. She patted Misha on the neck to reassure her. "Ribbon or no ribbon, we'll do our best."

As they walked back to find the adults, Jo noticed a handful of competitors wearing whistles around their necks. Most of them were older men wearing big cowboy hats and ankle length dusters. They looked like cowboys from the Old West. There was a teenaged boy in the mix. He wore a short denim coat and a worn-out saggy hat.

"It looks like you're the only girl in the competition," Todd told Jo.

"Two girls," said Jo. "Me and Misha."

She wondered if the others were as good as she was at blowing a clean note.

"Don't worry about the rest of them," said a familiar voice. "You got the best herding dog in Colorado."

Jo turned and saw Mr. Wills. "You came!"

"If you thought I was going to stay home when the world's greatest dog and her owner competed you're wrong! Now before you go out there, make sure you warm that whistle in your hands. I don't want you missing a single note."

"Okay, Mr. Wills."

Mr. Wills shook hands with her family.

Jo's parents came over and knelt down in front of her and Misha.

"Have fun," said Charlie.

"We will," said Jo.

"We love you," said Anne.

"Not now, mom! Don't get all mushy on me."

"Well, we do!"

"I know," smiled Jo. "Now go sit in the bleachers. We got it."

Jo watched her family as they climbed up and sat on one of the temporary bleachers arranged outside a pasture. To the left of the pasture was a pen holding a small herd of cows for the competition. To the right of the pasture Jo saw an open gate leading to a corral

A few minutes passed. An announcer stepped up to a podium set up in the back of a pickup truck parked next to the bleachers. Three judges sat on the tailgate. There was a loudspeaker standing on the hood of the truck so everyone could hear.

"Will the owners and their dogs make their way to the front of the podium?" said the announcer.

Jo and Misha entered the pasture and followed the cowboys.

The announcer looked down from his podium and bent his neck. "You there, young lady. Come to the front so we can see you. I need to explain the rules."

A few of the cowboys stepped aside for Jo and Misha as they wiggled up to the front.

"That's better," said the announcer. He made a quick count. "We have ten competitors today. We got sixty cows?" he called to a cowboy working the gate to the pen.

The cowboy gave the announcer a "thumbs up".

"Good. Now let me explain the rules," said the announcer. "We start with an empty pasture. One of our cowboys over in the pen will cut six head of cattle loose in the pasture. When the pen gate closes behind those cows the clock starts.

"The goal of today's event is for the owner and his dog to herd those cows together and drive them into the corral. When the cattle are in the corral, the owner closes the gate and the clock stops.

"Your time will count for fifty percent of your score. The other fifty is tallied from your use of whistles, audible commands and hand signals.

"We ask that all owners keep their dogs leashed to a rail until it's your turn. Okay, cowboys, and uh, cowgirl, let's start the Steamboat Springs Annual Invitational Herding Competition! May the best dog win!"

The announcer drew a name scrawled on a piece of paper from a fish bowl. "First up we got Rowdy Yankins and his dog Skillet."

The cowboy and his dog stood close to the fence as the others left the pasture. The gate opened from the pen and six cows meandered in. The gate closed.

Rowdy Yankins blew on a whistle and his dog took off running to the far end of the pasture where the cows had huddled together.

"He's got it easy," Grandpa Henry told Mr. Wills. "Cows are already sitting pretty."

Everyone watched as the dog moved the cows together towards the corral. Rowdy Yankins used mostly voice commands. Skillet turned the herd back towards the pens and Rowdy used his whistle for new instructions.

"Dog missed his cue," said Mr. Wills. "That'll cost him some time."

One by one, dogs and their owners were called into the pasture for their turns. Jo watched anxiously as gates opened and closed. When the others finished their times, the small crowd in the bleachers applauded them for their skills and hard work.

Jo looked down at Misha. "Stay with me, girl. Don't pay attention."

Misha looked up at her. She seemed to be grinning.

"Yes, it is fun!" Jo laughed.

At last it was their turn.

"And now Number Six," said the announcer. "Josephine Wilson and her dog Misha."

Jo drew a deep breath and said softly, "Here we go, baby girl!" She patted Misha on the head. Jo glanced up into the bleachers and saw all the family with big smiles and thumbs up. She unsnapped Misha's leash from a railing of the fence and entered the pasture with her.

Misha stayed close to Jo as they waited for the cattle to be led into the pen. The cattle quietly roamed in and spread out near the far end of the pasture. One of them was the queen they saw earlier. White Eye!

"Let's show her who's boss," Jo said. Misha looked from Jo to the cattle. She was ready.

"Way up Misha, way up," Jo called out.

Misha dashed off to the far side of the pasture moving left of the cattle. Their clock was ticking.

Misha ran up to White Eye first and moved her away from the back fence towards the others. White Eye obliged. The cattle moved together in a tight herd. Jo watched intently. Misha sat on her heels, staring down the cattle. They didn't move.

Jo hurried towards the corral gate and blew two sharp whistle notes that told Misha to "circle up". Misha stood and moved the cattle towards her. White Eye got out of the herd and tried to run off. Jo blew a new whistle note; Number Six, the hardest note to find. It sounded perfect.

Misha sprang towards the cow and redirected it back to the herd. White Eye hesitated. Misha ran up and stared her in the eyes and White Eye nodded her head, returning to the front of the herd facing Jo.

Jo blew a new note. The cattle trotted towards her, Misha at their heels. Jo stood to the side of the open gate, circled her arm high in the air and blew a new high note on the whistle.

Misha prodded the herd into the corral. When the cows were inside, Misha ran out and sat at Jo's heels. Jo slammed the gate shut behind them and the clocked stopped.

Jo tossed her ball cap in the air and hugged Misha.

Grandpa Henry and Mr. Wills looked at the time clock by the truck.

"Jo and Misha took the lead!" shouted Mr. Wills.

The Wilsons, Marshalls and Penners were jumping up and down in the bleachers.

The announcer picked up his microphone. "Careful there, folks. Those bleachers might break!"

Everyone sat down and laughed.

Jo and Misha left the pasture and Jo snapped the leash back on Misha.

"You did great, baby girl! Just great!" said Jo.

She didn't bother looking at her score. Jo had promised herself she would teach Misha to be the best herding dog ever and she knew she was.

Other cowboys ran their dogs against the cows. The last one in was the older boy in the denim jacket. He had a good group of obedient cows. He gave good commands. His whistle blew clean. When he was done, the announcer picked up his microphone.

"Ladies and gentlemen, I am proud to announce the winner of this year's competition. Will Josephine Wilson and her dog Misha please come to the podium to collect your prize!"

With that Jo led Misha up to the judges. She was handed a blue ribbon and a check for five hundred dollars.

Everyone in the stands was clapping. The Wilsons, Marshalls, and Penners were clapping the loudest with Todd doing his famous two finger whistle.

Jo bent down and tucked the blue ribbon in Misha's collar.

"My, oh my," said Mr. Wills. "Unbelievable!"

"That's some dog," said Grandpa Henry.

"And Jo is some girl," said Mr. Wills.

CHAPTER 23

CHANGING SEASONS

The cold and snow of an early winter set in.

On Thanksgiving the Wilsons, Grandpa Henry and Grandma Elizabeth gathered at the Marshall ranch for turkey.

With his father's help Todd had butchered and cleaned a turkey the day before.

"Did he have a name?" John Marshall asked.

"Number two," said Todd.

The Christmas Pageant was next. Sally Stroud had left the chorus, complaining of a sore throat. Jo volunteered to change places with her and Sally had her dream role as the Angel of the Lord. Her voice came back the day before the actual event.

Everyone skipped the Denver Stock Show that year. Curly didn't have to compete anymore and the road to Denver was trapped in a blizzard.

The February Box Supper raised three hundred dollars for the school. Luke bought Jo's dessert box for twenty dollars. It was a school record for a cherry pie topped with cream cheese. Luke raised his money from shoveling snow all winter. Matt Turner decided he didn't like Hannah anymore and bid on another girl's dessert. For weeks afterward Jo listened to Hannah complaining about how useless boys were.

Jo noticed Misha was walking a little slower than before. The hard winter was taking its toll. Misha's muscles and bones were getting older but she never passed up an opportunity to race Jo to the barn in the snow or follow her on a short horseback ride with Hannah.

When spring arrived, Todd and Luke picked up their ropes again and practiced their team-roping. Luke had joined Todd's turkey-raising firm as a partner and found a grocery store to carry their "Ranch grown fine fowls."

Hannah started her jumping again with Lily. Jo didn't see her as much as she used to. They weren't growing apart as friends; they were just growing older with different directions in life.

One night Jo asked her mom, "Would you and Claire be such good sisters if you didn't live next door to each other?"

"I think so," said Anne. "I would hope so. When we were kids we promised each other we would always be friends and sisters no matter what."

"Me and Hannah made a promise like that," said Jo. "All the way to the moon and back."

Anne took Jo outside to the porch. She pointed up at the sky. "There's your moon," she said. "See those three stars in a line to the right? One of them is Hannah."

"What are the other two stars?"

"Well," said Anne tenderly. "I think one of them is you and one of them is Misha."

Jo rubbed her chin and pondered. "Will the stars always be there?"

"They've been there since before we were born and they'll be there after we're gone," said her mother.

Jo nodded as she understood. "Always and forever. All the way to the moon and back."

They spent a half hour on the porch picking out stars for everyone in the family. Jo found stars for the horses too.

CHAPTER 24

MISHA AND THE COYOTE

It was a good day for a ride. School would be out in a week for the summer.

Jo got Sundance's corral cleaned, fed the horses, and replaced the water in their drinking troughs.

Misha thought she was helping too. She sniffed the barn floor, checked out the corrals and chased away a rabbit that wandered by. When she was satisfied she found a pile of loose hay and lay down.

By the time Jo was done with her chores, Sundance had finished his hay and grain. She put a halter on him and looped the rope around the middle rail of the fence and started to brush him.

"I think today will be a good day for a ride. Don't you?" Jo said as she combed his tail.

Jo got her saddle, placed it on his back and tightened the girth. She put the reins over Sundance's head and called for Misha.

"Let's check out the pond for ducks and see the baby calves. I bet they are getting big and fat." Jo tied the herding whistle around her neck. "I'm working on a new song," she told Misha. "Mr. Wills suggested it so I'll stay in practice but won't confuse you."

Misha turned her head and cocked her ears.

"The name of the song?" smiled Jo. "'*Mary Had A Little Lamb*.' You ready?"

Jo jumped on Sundance and rode up to her mom working in the flower bed in front of the house. Misha followed close at the horse's heels.

"We're going to the West Douglas and maybe ride The Fingers," she said.

Her mom waved back. "I'll tell your father. Have a good ride. Be careful. "

"I will," said Jo. "Besides, I got Misha with me."

The air was cool and crisp. Jo was glad she had a sweat-shirt to put on.

Misha darted throughout the scrub oak stopping now and then, looking through the many thin oak trunks and low branches for varmints.

Every now and then, Sundance would stop and look at something Jo could not see. Jo knew to pay close attention to her animals. They had eyes and instincts she would never have.

"It can't be anything but a bird!" Jo thought to herself as Misha jumped back and forth across the stream that followed the dirt road to the pond and open grass area.

When they arrived at the pond there were two ducks swimming quietly on its surface, the sun making dancing sparkles on the water.

Sundance stopped to watch them and Misha jumped in the water for a swim. The ducks turned and swam in the opposite direction to keep their distance from Misha.

Cows and their babies were grazing in the grass close to the pond near the hills the family called The Fingers. The hills extended from the base of the mountain and looked like three long thick fingers on a hand. The valleys in between were steep in spots with lots of scrub oak that made riding in them hard.

Jo raised her whistle to work on her new song. She called to Misha. "Listen to this!" Misha seemed to smile as she blew the notes perfectly.

Jo turned Sundance north and headed towards The Fingers, blowing on her whistle as she rode. Misha took the lead, trotting ahead of Sundance. When they reached the foot of the first Finger, Jo put her whistle away and leaned forward in her saddle to help Sundance up the hill. When they reached the top, she stopped Sundance so he could catch his breath.

Jo looked east at the growing town below. "Boy, Sundance! We can almost see Kansas from here."

Misha started smelling the grama and wild flowers covering the ground. Jo turned Sundance around and headed back down the hill, going in a zig-zagging motion so it wouldn't be hard on his legs.

The three had just made it to the flat ground at the bottom when Misha and Sundance froze, their ears up, staring ahead.

"Uh-oh!" Jo said under her breath as she saw the gray animal. "A coyote!"

Misha was off like a bolt of lightning.

Jo screamed for Misha to come, but Misha ran on. Jo kicked Sundance in his side to get him to a fast canter and galloped after Misha. She remembered her whistle and started to blow the tone for "Misha – come".

But Misha didn't listen this time. She was on a mission to get the coyote. Coyotes would taunt Misha from time to time but usually nothing came of it. Misha might chase one for a short time but the coyotes always ran away until she dropped her short chase. But this coyote was different. It was bigger than most, its fur gnarled and dirty. It wasn't afraid of Misha in the least. The coyote stopped and turned to face her.

"No Misha! No!" Jo shouted.

The coyote had its tail fluffed out, the back hair on its shoulders was standing up and its teeth where showing.

Misha didn't back down. She too had hair standing up. Her head was low and teeth showing as she growled and slowly moved towards the coyote.

Sundance stopped in his tracks. He wouldn't take another step forward. Jo took a quick look around to make sure there wasn't another coyote lurking somewhere. Sometimes they travelled in pairs or small packs. But she could only see the one in her path. Sundance started stepping from one leg to the other, jostling Jo up and down, as if ready to buck her.

Jo had never seen an animal move so quickly. The coyote charged head-on at Misha, head low, mouth open as it aimed for Misha's throat. Misha backed away and flung herself to the coyote's side, snapping and biting at its hindquarters as the coyote turned and slashed at Misha's hind leg with her teeth. The dirt of the trail turned up into a small cloud around them as the scene turned into a fuzz of flying fur and deep growls.

Sundance raised up in the air now. Jo slid off his side and pulled on the reins with all of her might to face the horse towards home. She slapped Sundance hard on the rear.

"Go Sundance! Run home! Get help!"

Sundance ran in the direction of home, empty stirrups flapping against his sides, the reins swinging wildly around his neck.

Jo saw a thick stick on the ground and grabbed it up. She turned and faced the dog fight. She had to help Misha, she just had to. Misha was only a dog. She didn't have the killing instinct of the mad coyote. Jo raised the stick in the air and ran into the fray, swiping at the coyote over and over again as it seemed to twirl out of reach, tossing Misha ahead of her. Blood flew all around her as she swung at the coyote over and over again, distracting it only a little as the coyote lunged at Misha again and again and Misha fought back.

Jo was terrified. She found herself screaming at the top of her lungs as she poked and smacked at the gray coyote to go away. A few times she saw the coyote's open mouth, inches away from her own legs as it snapped and growled and salivated. Was there no stopping it? She saw Misha's eyes, wild with a mix of fright and anger as she bravely fought back.

"Go away!" Go away! Go away!" Jo screamed at the coyote.

But it would not stop.

Sundance knew what to do. He ran like the wind towards home. As he neared the barn at a full gallop, Bell and Checkers came running out from the barn into their corral and started to buck and nicker as they ran back and forth along the corral fence.

Charlie was working in the tack room cleaning saddles when he heard all the commotion coming from the corral. He ran out and saw the horses.

"Oh no... Sundance alone. Where is Jo?" Charlie yelled to his wife, still in the flower bed by the house. "Anne! Come quick! Jo's in trouble!"

He ran inside the barn and grabbed his hunting rifle off the wall. His wife met him at the truck, seeing Sundance without a rider. They jumped in the truck.

"Jo said she was taking Sundance up the West Douglas towards the Three Fingers," Anne said.

"Is Misha with her?"

"Yes."

"That's some consolation," Charlie said as he punched the gas pedal and drove up the winding dirt road.

They rolled their windows down, looking in all directions, thinking the worse of things as the truck bounced over deep ruts.

"If I drive any faster, I'll flip the truck over," Charlie complained.

"Remember the big cat?" Anne finally said.

"I remember," said Charlie. "The bear, too."

The truck cleared a stand of trees.

Anne pointed across the pond towards the flats below The Fingers. "There she is! Misha's got a coyote!"

Charlie stomped his foot on the gas pedal, the truck's tires spinning in the soft dirt of the field towards the battle.

Anne's eyes never strayed from the fight. "Jo's got a big stick! But that coyote won't back off!" she said.

Charlie slammed on the brakes twenty feet from the fight and jumped out of the truck, rifle in hand.

Anne leapt from her side of the truck, yelling and jumping in the air, arms flapping at the coyote as she moved forward.

The coyote finally backed away, turned and started to run.

Charlie raised his rifle, took aim and fired one clean shot.

The coyote fell head over heels in the grass, stopped dead in its tracks.

Anne ran up to her daughter. Jo's hands were swollen red from squeezing the big stick. There was blood on her shirt.

"Are you bit?" Anne asked.

"I don't think so," Jo said. "But Misha is!"

They looked at Misha. She had dropped to the ground, breathing heavily on her side, eyes closed. Anne and Jo dropped to their knees alongside her.

Jo couldn't stop herself from crying now. "That coyote, it tore her up bad, mom!"

"Charlie, grab the first aid kit from the truck," Anne called.

Charlie hurried to the truck and found the kit behind the seat. "Looks like old Misha's pretty tore up," he said as he knelt beside them.

"Will she be alright?" Jo asked.

Anne opened the kit and found a pair of scissors and rolls of gauze bandages. "First thing is we have to stop the bleeding," she said. She started snipping away strips and handing them to Jo. "Wrap Misha's legs," said Anne. "Nice and tight."

"Will it hurt?" Jo said.

Anne looked down at Misha. Her breathing was fainter now. “Hurry, Jo. Just do as I say.”

Charlie rose up with his rifle and walked over to the coyote. He poked at its carcass with the barrel.

“This skin will be a good trophy for Jo and Misha,” he said to himself. Charlie grabbed the dead coyote by the tail and dragged it to the back of the truck. “It might have rabies. The vet will want to examine it.” He threw the lifeless body in the back of the truck.

“Thanks for killing that thing!” Jo cried as she wrapped Misha’s leg. “We have to save Misha!”

Mrs. Wilson pulled square patches of band aids from the kit and applied them to Misha’s body and face. “Let’s get her in the truck,” she called to Charlie.

He set the rifle in the truck and picked Misha up off the dusty patch of earth marked with paw and foot prints. Misha didn’t flinch. As he carried her, Jo pet Misha’s unmarked hindquarters.

"I’m here, Misha. Every step of the way,” she said.

Her parents looked at her, worry on their faces.

“Must have been a heck of a fight,” Charlie said.

“It was,” said Jo. “I never saw anything like it. How bad is Misha?”

“I won’t lie,” said Charlie as he carefully laid Misha on the seat. “She’s pretty torn up.”

Jo jumped in the truck and carefully rested Misha’s head on her lap.

Anne slid in next to her and put her arm on Jo’s shoulder. “Keep talking to her. Let her know you’re here.”

“Let’s get Misha to the vet,” said Charlie as he fired up the truck and spun away from the scene of the fight.

“Why did the coyote come at us like that?” Jo asked. “They always left us alone before.”

“We never know what’s in the mind of a wild creature,” said Anne.

Jo looked over her shoulder at the dead coyote. "It was mean," she said. She gently stroked Misha's fur, ignoring the tears that ran down her cheeks. "Lord, please don't let her die."

Charlie drove as fast as the speed limit allowed to town. It seemed longer than normal. "How is Misha doing?" he asked several times.

"She's still breathing," Jo would say as she touched Misha with gentle strokes.

Twenty minutes later Charlie pulled up to the vet's office. He carefully lifted Misha off the seat of the truck. Anne went ahead and opened the door. Jo walked alongside Misha holding her paw.

Doc Brown followed Charlie and Misha down the hall into a small operating room with a cold metal table. Charlie set her down carefully. Doc Brown listened as Jo told him everything that had happened.

"You are a very brave girl," he told Jo.

"Not as brave as Misha but I had to do something," Jo said, holding Misha's paw.

"Your father and I have work to do. I think it best if you wait with Jo in the waiting room," Doc Brown told Mrs. Wilson. "This will take some time."

Jo bent over Misha and gave her one last hug. She whispered in her ear. "Stay with me Misha. I don't want to lose you."

There was a slight movement under Misha's closed eyes.

"She heard you," said Anne as she led Jo from the room.

After a few minutes in the waiting room, Anne borrowed a phone from the receptionist and called the Marshalls with the unfortunate news.

"How is Misha doing?"

"It doesn't look good."

"How is Jo taking it?" said Claire.

"She's being brave," said Anne.

"We'll be there as soon as we can," said Claire.

Anne and Jo found a seat and waited quietly. Long seconds turned to long minutes.

The Marshall family arrived thirty minutes later. Hannah hurried up to Jo and sat beside her as they hugged. "Misha will be okay," Hannah said.

"She's always been one tough girl," said Todd. "Can we go see her?" he asked his parents.

"Have a seat," ordered his dad. "They'll let us know."

"I called Grandpa and Grandma," said Claire. "They'll be here as soon as they can."

When the grandparents arrived, Jo recounted the bloody fight for everyone.

"And you jumped in with a stick?" said Grandma Elizabeth. "I never heard such a thing!"

"I had to do something!" Jo said. "It wasn't a fair fight."

"Sometimes we forget that we still live in a wild country," said her grandpa.

"You're just lucky it wasn't a big cat!" Todd told Jo.

"A coyote was bad enough," said Hannah. She squeezed Jo's hand. "I don't think I could have done what you did!"

The family sat in the waiting room for almost an hour. It was getting dark outside.

"I can't sit here and do nothing," said Claire. "How about I walk down to the café and get us all something to eat?"

"I'm not hungry," said Jo.

"Do they make chile dogs?" said Todd.

"I believe they do," said his mother.

"Hamburgers?" said Hannah.

"And soda pop in glass bottles."

"I suppose I could eat something," decided Jo.

"I'll go with you," offered Anne.

Claire and Anne headed out the door.

Uncle John took Grandpa Henry and Todd outside to look at the coyote carcass in the back of his son's truck.

Before the mothers returned, Doc Brown and Charlie Wilson came down the hallway from the operating room.

"What's the verdict?" said Hannah's father.

Doc Brown scratched his head and spoke softly. "The good news is I ran a rabies test and there doesn't seem to be anything there. Misha has a broken leg and several deep cuts and bites I managed to close. She'll be on heavy antibiotics for a few weeks. She'll need plenty of bed rest during her recovery."

"But she'll live?" said Jo.

"She'll live just fine," smiled the veterinarian. "The best medicine for her now is your love and attention."

Jo, Hannah and Todd joined hands and jumped up and down, cheering.

"Easy now, kids. This is a hospital," laughed the vet.

"Is Misha awake?" said Jo.

"She's awake and alert."

"Can I see her?" begged Jo.

Everyone paused to listen to the sound of a dog's high bark echoing down the hallway.

"If Misha's bark tells me anything, she's been asking for you."

Jo ran down the hall to the operating room followed by Hannah and Todd.

Charlie was there with Misha, supporting her on the steel table as the kids barged in.

At the sight of Jo, Misha couldn't stop barking. She seemed to be sharing the coyote fight with Jo in great detail.

Jo gently hugged Misha, petting her constantly. Todd and Hannah looked on, admiring the love between them.

"Misha is the best cow dog ever!" said Todd.

Doc Brown came in and stood by Jo. She paused long enough to give him a great big hug around his waist.

"Thank you for saving Misha's life," Jo said.

Doc Brown shook his head. "All I did was stitch her up. I'd say you're the hero today."

"You mean me and Misha," said Jo.

The mothers returned to the clinic with food and everyone laughed and shared the day's events in the lobby with the kind doctor who sat patiently and sipped on an ice cold soda pop.

"This is one of those days you never forget," reminded the doctor.

Grandma Elizabeth pulled her husband up from his seat. "Looks like everyone is going to be okay," she said. "Time to get you home. Its past your bedtime."

"Just a little longer?" said Grandpa Henry. "Me and Todd have one more chile dog left."

CHAPTER 25

THE RECOVERY

On the way home from Dr. Brown's office Misha was very still, her head resting on Jo's lap, eyes closed but once in a while her tail would move as if to say "Thank you".

"Mom and Dad," Jo decided. "Misha has lived a full life. I think now she should just hang out around the barns and maybe take a slow run with Sundance sometime, but no more working the cows."

"That sounds like a good plan," said her mother.

Jo rested her hand gently on Misha's back. "Maybe there's a 4-H project about healing a dog back to health after a fight with a coyote," she said.

"Maybe there is." Charlie said with a smile.

He drove past the gate towards their house. When the truck stopped and the doors opened, Sundance trotted to the fence in his corral and put his head over the railing as if to ask, "How is Misha?"

Jo looked at Sundance and said, "Misha will be fine. She will be out in the barn in no time. I promise."

Sundance bobbed his head as if he understood her.

Charlie carried Misha into the house. Jo ran ahead and moved Misha's dog bed from the den into a cozy corner in the kitchen.

"She'll like it in here," Jo told her parents as she pulled a soft blanket from the linen closet and covered the top of the bed.

Charlie laid Misha on it. Misha raised her head slightly.

"She's in a lot of pain," said Anne. "The medication is starting to wear off."

There was a tap on the kitchen door and there stood the Marshall family.

"It's been a long day for you," said John Marshall. "Todd and I will feed and water the animals." He and Todd headed for the barn.

Claire took a seat in the kitchen with Charlie and Anne. Hannah joined Jo next to Misha on the floor and watched her.

"No tears or anything?" said Hannah.

"I'm too tired to cry and why would I anyway? I'm okay and Misha will get better in no time."

Hannah touched the bandages on Misha's leg. "We just have to make sure she stays off this bad leg."

"I'll watch her day and night if I have to," Jo said.

Her mother stood up and turned on the oven. "May as well heat up a pie for everyone," she said. "You girls want ice cream with it?"

"If it's vanilla," said Jo.

"Vanilla it is!" said her mother.

Hannah shook her head and laughed.

"What's so funny?" Jo asked.

"Back to vanilla, I see. Some things never change."

Jo rubbed her nose in Misha's fur, listening to her slow steady breathing and the soft ticking of her heart. She whispered quietly, "I love you, baby girl. Sleep tight."

CHAPTER 26

AFTER THE SUMMER

The days of summer went by quickly. By the time August arrived, Misha was walking almost as good as new with just a slight limp in her left back leg. She was always ready to help Jo in the barn. She enjoyed the walks they took that added strength to her legs and body.

School was just around the corner and it was going to be a new year in many ways.

Jo was still going to the Woodmen school. Hannah and Luke were starting Junior High and would be joining Todd who was in his second year. Todd had found a new sport at school – football. Luke wanted to play, too.

She would still see Hannah and Todd at the 4-H meetings and their homes. She would still be riding the horses with Hannah whenever they could.

Jo was glad Misha would be there to walk her to the bus stop in the morning and be waiting for her when she got home.

Jo and Misha headed out for a late afternoon walk. Jo had decided to keep Sundance in the barn until Misha was able to keep up again.

"Give it a few more weeks," Jo promised Misha.

School started again. The building seemed smaller than the previous year and the kids seemed younger than Jo remembered. She didn't talk much on the bus ride home anymore. Sally had gone on to stardom with Hannah and Luke at the new school.

The foothills were alive with color. The first Saturday of October arrived with spectacular fall colors in the aspen trees. Their shades of gold, red, and orange were replacing the hint of summer's green leaves. The scrub oaks had already turned from orange to brown.

Jo dressed quickly and hurried downstairs to the kitchen.

"Are you ready for the fall round-up?" asked Anne.

"Misha's ready, too!" said Jo. "Her legs are good as new."

"Your father is out in the barn," said Anne. "You better hurry up."

Jo found Charlie in the barn with the horses. "Sundance is saddled. I just have to get a bit on Bell," he said. "We'll ride over to help Uncle John this morning, then he'll help us with our herd this afternoon."

"What about Todd and Hannah?"

"They'll be there. Todd bought himself a new roping saddle."

"I can't wait to catch up with Hannah about her new school," said Jo.

"I'll bet you can't. Don't spend too much time talking. We have cattle to move."

"I know, dad."

They mounted the horses and rode to the Marshall ranch. Misha trotted ahead of them, her legs moving in sync with an easy stride.

"Misha looks good," said Charlie.

"You know how she loves herding cows," said Jo.

Charlie smiled. "Did you bring your whistle just in case you need it?"

Jo pulled it out from under her coat and showed it to him.

Uncle John, Todd and Hannah were waiting for them at the back gate. Uncle John had a puzzled look on his face.

"What's wrong?" said Charlie.

"No cows," said Uncle John. "I found a section of fence down in the back. I think they went up the jeep road towards The Fingers to eat on the shrubs and plants or down along the creek for the wild flowers." He didn't take long to make his decision. "Jo and Hannah, you ride down and shake the stray cows and their calves out from the bushes by the creek. Todd, you pick them up and lead them back here. Charlie and I will search The Fingers."

The kids turned their horses and trotted off.

Misha tried to take the lead but Smokey wanted to run. Todd let him as he waved his rope in the air swinging at branches along the path.

"I found some," Todd shouted back to the girls as he pulled Smokey to a stop.

Jo looked in the dense bushes and saw the lazy faces of a few dozen cows and their calves caught up in the roots.

"It'll take all day to chase them out," Todd complained.

"No, it won't," said Jo. She looked down at Misha. "Go get, 'em, baby girl!"

Misha raced into the thick brush. One by one, cows and calves started appearing on the road. Every now and then Jo could see Misha as her head popped through the trees behind the tail of a delivered cow.

Todd and Hannah trotted further down the trail into a grove of pine trees and drove more cows out.

Jo laughed and listened to them as they herded.

"Come-on baby, silly cow come this way, so cow, so cow, come on baby, let's go."

The snap of branches and the bawling of cows and calves accompanied their voices as they broke into the clearing.

Uphill at The Fingers, John and Charlie found the rest of the scattered herd and turned them downhill towards the Marshall ranch. The unwilling cows and calves kicked up their heels and bawled as they trotted home.

The kids met the fathers near the open gap in the fence.

"You girls and Misha push the cattle to the pond for a drink. We can count them there," said Uncle John.

Jo raised her whistle and blew a high note. Misha ran to the back of the cows and prodded them forward through the downed fence towards the pond.

Uncle John pulled a pair of pliers from his saddle bag. "Uncle Charlie and I will fix this fence. Todd, you ride outside the fence line and see if we have any strays. We'll wait for your return before we seal the fence."

Todd smiled and waved his new rope high in the air as he galloped off. "Yes sir!"

"He's a regular cowboy," laughed Uncle Charlie.

"Sometimes too much," said Uncle John.

Todd didn't find any strays. His dad and uncle bound the wire fence behind him and they rode together to the pond. Satiated cattle looked up at them briefly, wondering if there was food at hand.

"Okay," ordered Uncle John. "Let's get our count. Todd, I want you to run the cows and their calves out one at a time. I'm sure the calves will follow their mothers so take it nice and slow. If the herd breaks out together, we'll have to start our count all over."

"Misha can do it with me and Hannah," said Jo. "Let Todd run the counts back to the barn."

"Okay, we can try that," said Uncle John.

Jo turned to Hannah. "You park right and I'll park left. We'll let Misha push the cows between us one at a time."

"If one gets behind me, I'll chase it to the moon and back and get them back in the herd," said Hannah.

Jo smiled. Hannah had remembered their solemn promise.

"What? You think I don't remember?" said Hannah. "I'll always remember what we share. We're not just cousins. We're more than friends. We're as close to being sisters as our own moms."

"To the moon and back then," said Jo.

"Further if we have to," Hannah nodded. She tucked her ball cap down on her forehead. Jo did the same.

"Bring up those cows," Jo called to her father.

One by one cows and calves slipped between the girls as Uncle John counted.

"You look like you're counting money at the feed store," said Charlie.

"I am," said John. "But this money's still on the hoof."

"We do pretty good for gentleman farmers," Charlie laughed.

"That we do, doc. That we do."

A cow rushed through the gauntlet. Jo blew her whistle. Misha headed off the cow and led it back for the count.

"Got it," Uncle John said.

Misha freed the cow up and ran along it until Todd picked it up in the pasture and ushered it to the holding corral. Misha ran back to the gauntlet between the girls.

"This is better than counting sheep in my sleep," Hannah laughed.

After the last cow and calf passed by, Uncle John tallied his count.

"Looks like we lost three this winter," he told Charlie.

There were a dozen cows and calves lingering outside the corral. They came so fast Todd couldn't keep up with them.

Jo saw the crowding and looked down at Misha. "Way up, way up, Misha."

She whistled once and Misha trotted towards the cows and calves, darting quickly to the right then left of the herd driving it towards the corral.

"What did that last whistle mean?" Hannah asked.

"Gate," said Jo. "If she wanted Misha could take a cow past the corral, through the barn, over your front lawn, into the kitchen and park it right in front of the television for The Ed Sullivan Show. Want me to show you?"

"That I would like to see," said Hannah.

Uncle John rode up. "The last thing we need is our cows coming home to watch television. Next thing you know they'll be swinging their hips to Elvis Presley. You girls ride next store and tell your mothers we're coming for lunch with appetites and attitudes before we count the Wilson Herefords."

Jo and Hannah galloped off to the Wilson ranch with Misha in their draft.

"Will you look at that dog run?" Uncle John said.

"She's the best," said Charlie.

Anne had made potato and leek soup and carrot cake. The girls filled their bowls and went to the front porch. Hannah told Jo all about Junior High.

"We have five minutes between classes. Science is my favorite class. History is okay but I have to write a twenty page term paper about the Civil War and one of its battles."

"You should get Luke to help you," said Jo. "He loves that stuff. What about English?"

"Too much reading. But I picked a book out to remind me of you."

"What is it?" said Jo.

"Why, it's *LITTLE WOMEN*, Josephine." Hannah smiled. She went inside to get more soup.

Todd passed his sister in the doorway and sat next to Jo. He had three slices of carrot cake balanced on top of each other.

"How's good ole Woodmen School?" he asked.

"Boring," Jo said as she took a bite of her own cake. "It is so quiet without Hannah."

"One more year and you won't be considered a kid anymore," Todd said. "Not that I think you're a kid."

"Why do you say that?"

"Heck," Todd said. "You and Misha won at Steamboat. You rope and herd cattle. You two faced mountain lions, bears and coyotes. That ain't kid stuff. You're not that skinny scarecrow I knew two years ago."

Misha pushed her way through the kitchen door and put her head in Jo's lap.

"What does she want?" Todd asked.

"Affection," said Jo.

"Typical girl," Todd sighed. "Too hard to figure out."

The afternoon round-up at the Wilson ranch went smoothly. Once again Misha was the star as she listened to Jo's commands. She darted in and out of the herd, nipping at the heels of disobedient cows when needed.

"Best herding dog in Colorado," Charlie Wilson said with pride.

Claire joined Anne in the Wilson kitchen and they cooked up a pan full of biscuits and gravy for their hungry and tired part-time cowboys and cowgirls.

"You know where I live," Hannah said to Jo as they ate. "I'm just down the road. Never far away. Never too far. You remember that."

"I do," said Jo.

Hannah slipped on her coat and gave Jo a final hug. "I love you."

"I love you, too," Jo said.

"To the moon?" Hannah asked. There was sadness in her voice.

"And back," promised Jo.

After the Marshalls rode off towards home, Charlie turned to his daughter. "Josephine, there's a nice October breeze outside. What say we take the horses and Misha for an evening walk for a last cool down?"

Jo tapped her ball cap on her head and followed him outside.

Charlie and Jo opened up their horses down the long dirt trail behind the property. They finally pulled up on the reins and waited for Misha to catch up. Misha sat at their feet, her tongue hanging as she breathed hard.

"When we got Misha, she was already grown," Charlie said. "Let's try something new." He slid off Bell, reached down and picked Misha up. "Scuttle back a hair," he told Jo.

Jo wriggled back in her saddle and Charlie placed Misha in front of her. "I don't see that it's necessary for Misha to run everywhere when she can ride just as easy," said her father.

Jo patted Misha on the head, clicked her heels and led Sundance down the trail. As they rode, Misha's head bobbed ahead of her, smelling the grass and searching for any sign of a rabbit or squirrel that might appear.

"You know something, dad?" Jo said as they reached an overlook displaying the lights of a growing city below.

"What's that?"

"I'm glad we live where we do. I know this coming year is going to be different, that's for sure. But I have Misha and Sundance and you and mom. That will never change."

Her father smiled and nodded.

Jo patted Sundance on the neck and helped Misha to the ground. "Misha still has her legs under her. She was born to the earth. I know she's getting old, but she's always been free. I don't want to take that from her."

"I understand," said her father.

"We all need to run free as long as we can," Jo said.

"As long as we can," said her father.

Misha trotted ahead of them. Something caught her eye. Her head turned and her ears perked up. Soon she was running like a thin pencil line after a deer.

"Isn't she amazing?" Jo said as she watched the best dog in the world run like the wind.

RECIPES IN THE BOOK

The majority of these recipes are from Cow Country Gourmet, an out-of-print cookbook written by my mother Marian L. Wolfe.
The cookbook was a collection of recipes the family knew and loved.
The remaining recipes are from friends and family members I received over the years.

- Terry Wolfe

CHAPTER 9
THE BIG CAT IS BACK

CHILI

Heat 3 pounds of ground beef cook until no red is showing
Add: 15 ounce can of tomato sauce
1 cup of water
1 teaspoon of tabasco
1 teaspoon of salt
3 tablespoons of chili powder
1 teaspoon of cayenne pepper
1 tablespoon of oregano
1 teaspoon of paprika
2 onions, chopped
Red peppers or chili pods, to taste
Garlic to taste
Simmer for 1 hour
**Add beans if desired, or serve over rice. Beans can be chili beans, pinto, red kidney beans or other.*

CHAPTER 11
THANKSGIVING

HOMEMADE EGG NOG

12 medium eggs
1 1/2 cups white sugar
4 cups whole milk
2 cups heavy cream
1 teaspoon ground nutmeg
1 teaspoon vanilla
Place egg yolks and sugar in a blender until the mix is thickened
Pour into a large bowl
Whisk in milk until sugar has completely dissolved
Sprinkle nutmeg and pour in the vanilla mix well
Chill until ready to serve
**Sprinkle with ground cinnamon over each glass or cup just*
Before serving.

CARROT COOKIES

1 cup butter
1 1/2 teaspoon vanilla
1 cup shortening
½ teaspoon of salt
¾ cup of sugar
2 cups flour
1 egg
2 teaspoons of baking power
1 cup cooked and mashed carrots
Blend butter and sugar. Add carrots and rest of ingredients
Drop by ½ teaspoons on greased cookie sheet
Bake 20 minutes at 350.
Glaze with orange icing while warm

Orange icing:
1 cup powdered sugar
4 tablespoons of orange juice with ½ teaspoon grated orange
Rind. Mix well and frost the cookies
Makes about 5 dozen.

GINGER SNAPS

¾ cup soft shortening
¼ cup molasses
2 cups of sifted flour
¼ teaspoon of salt
1 cup brown sugar (dark brown)
2 teaspoons of soda
1 tsp each of ginger, cinnamon and cloves
1 egg
Combine shortening, sugar, and egg in bowl. Beat until fluffy. Add molasses and stir well.
Sift dry ingredients and add to mixture.
Chill thoroughly (about 2 hours).
Shape in 1-inch balls and roll in granulated sugar.
Place 2 inches apart on greased baking sheet.
Bake at 350 for 12 to 15 minutes.

PECAN PIE

4 eggs
½ teaspoon of salt
2/3 cup sugar
1/3 cup melted butter
1 cup dark corn syrup
1 cup of pecans
1 tablespoon of flour
2 teaspoons of vanilla
Beat eggs slightly and add remaining ingredients. Mix well. Pour into unbaked pie crust and bake at 325 for 75 minutes.

PUMPKIN PIE

Filling:
One 15 ounce can of solid pumpkin (about 2 cups)
1 cup heavy cream
½ cup whole milk
2 large eggs
¾ cup packed light brown sugar
1 teaspoon of ground cinnamon
1 teaspoon of ground ginger
pinch of ground cloves
¼ teaspoon of salt
preheat oven
Line pie plate with foil.
Bake handmade pie crust in glass pie plate at 375 for 6 minutes
Fill pie shell with filling.
Bake in middle of oven for 45 to 50 mixtures, or until center is set.

CROISSANTS

1 package of yeast (active dry or compressed
1/3 cup of sugar
1 cup of warm water
1 egg
¾ cup of evaporated milk
5 cups of unsifted flour
1 1/2 tsp salt
¼ cup of butter melted and cooled
1 cup of firm butter, cold
1 egg beaten with 1 teaspoon of water
In bowl let yeast soften in warm water
Add milk, salt, sugar, egg and 1 cup of flour
Beat to make a smooth batter
Blend in melted butter
In a large bowl, cut the 1 cup of firm butter into remaining 4 cups of flour until butter particles are the size of beans
Pour yeast batter over top and carefully blend until all the flour is blended
Cover and refrigerate until well chilled, at least 4 hours or up to 4 days
Roll dough on a floured board and knead about 6 to 8 times.
Divide into 4 parts
Shape 1 part at a time and leave remainder covered and in refrigerator
Roll in circle, 15 3/4'inch in diameter, and using a sharp knife, cut like a pie into 8 equal pieces
Loosely roll each croissant toward the point, loosely
Cover rolls and let rise until double, about 2 hours
Brush lightly with beaten egg and water and bake at 325 degrees about 20 minutes.

SWEET POTATOES

*12 servings
1 cup unsalted butter, room temperature
1 cup packed golden brown sugar
1 1/2 teaspoon group nutmeg
12 yams (red-skinned sweet potatoes)
beat butter, sugar, and nutmeg until light and fluffy.
Preheat oven to 350
Peel and cube the yams and place in a baking dish
Cover them with the butter mixture and bake until done about 1 hour.

GREEN BEANS AND MUSHROOMS

2 pounds of fresh green beans, stem ends trimmed, removed
4 tablespoons butter
1 lb. button mushrooms stem trimmed and cut in half
2 shallots cut in ¼ rings
Steam green beans until crisp and tender (5 to 10 minutes). Heat butter over medium heat.
Add mushrooms and shallots
Season with salt and pepper
Cover and cook for 3 to 5 minutes, stirring occasionally. Uncover and cook, tossing occasionally until brown (8 -12 min).
Add green beans.
Cook until heated thoroughly.

BUTTERNUT SQUASH SOUP

Cut squash in half and clean out seeds
Bake butternut squash in oven with sprinkled brown sugar and a few pats of butter
Bake about 45 minutes at 350 or until done
Cool and peel skin off. Discard the skin
Put the squash in food processor with chicken broth to cover the squash
Add more to make it a soup
Add a pint of Half and Half or more to taste
**Add a pinch of curry and a pinch of nutmeg and serve.*

CHAPTER 12
THE CHRISTMAS PAGEANT

CANDY POPCORN BALLS

"Popcorn balls made with this caramel corn filled the Christmas stocking at Woodmen School for many, many years. I think every room mother had this recipe." - MLW

2 cups of sugar
¼ lb. butter
2 cups of corn syrup
1 teaspoon of vanilla
1/4 tsp salt
1 tall can of evaporated milk
Mix sugar and syrup together
Add salt
Let sit and cook until 250 degree on candy thermometer without further stirring.
When it reaches 350 degrees add milk and butter a little at a time so that mixture continues to a boil
Stir and cook until it reaches 242 to 244 degrees
Keep stirring, so that it doesn't burn
Add vanilla and pour at once over hot, freshly popped corn
Form into balls and serve.

CHAPTER 13
THE STOCK SHOW

HOT CHOCOLATE

The mix:
31/2 cups of sugar
2¼ cups of cocoa
1 teaspoon of salt
*Keep the above in an air container
Mix 2 tablespoons with a cup of hot milk
Sprinkle cinnamon and nutmeg and a few marshmallows on top (makes it magical).

CHOCOLATE CAKE

1 egg in a cup and fill with sour cream
3/4 teaspoon of baking powder
1 cup less 2 tablespoons of sugar
1 heaping tablespoon of cocoa
1 1l2 cups of flour
1 teaspoon of vanilla
3/4 teaspoon of soda
Beat sugar into egg and sour cream mixture
Add sifted dry ingredients, then vanilla
Pour into 8"x 8" square pan and bake at 350 degrees for 20 minutes.

CHERRY PIE

1 cup plus 1 tablespoon of sugar
1/4 teaspoon of salt
3 tablespoons of cornstarch
5 cups whole pitted cherries
1 teaspoon of fresh lemon juice
1/2 teaspoon vanilla extract
2 tablespoons of unsalted butter
1 tablespoon of milk
*preheat oven to 425f
Whisk 1 cup of sugar, cornstarch and salt in medium bowl to blend
Add in cherries, lemon juice, and vanilla, set aside
Roll out pie crust and place in glass pie plate
Put filling of cherries in and dot with butter. Place top crust on and pinch together
Or you can make a lattice top with strips of dough.
Place pie on baking sheet and bake for 15 minutes. Reduce to 375 degrees and bake until filling is bubbling and crust is golden brown (about an hour).

POTATO SALAD

1 1/2 lbs. potatoes peeled
1 1/2 cups of mayonnaise
1 tablespoon of white or cider vinegar
1 tablespoon of yellow mustard
1 cup of chopped celery
1 medium onion chopped
4 hard-cooked eggs chopped
Paprika to sprinkle on top
Place potatoes in boiling water. Cook 30 minutes or until tender.
Drain and cool and peel
Cut potatoes into cubes
Mix mayonnaise, vinegar, mustard, salt and pepper to taste in a bowl
Add potatoes, celery, onions, toss
Slice eggs and mix gently
Sprinkle with paprika
**Chill for at least 4 hours and serve.*

PINEAPPLE SAUCE

Two 8-ounce cans of crushed pineapple in juice
1 cup of brown sugar
2 tablespoons of lemon juice
1 teaspoon of mustard
Mix the above in a sauce pan over medium heat
Serve with warm ham

CHAPTER 19
LEARNING THE WHISTLE

OATMEAL COOKIES

3/4 cup of soft shortening
1 teaspoon of vanilla
1 cup firmly-packed brown sugar
1 cup sifted flour
1/2 cup granulated sugar
1 teaspoon salt
1 egg
1/2 teaspoon soda
1/4 cup water
3 cups of uncooked oats
Beat together shortening, sugars, egg, water and vanilla until creamy
Sift together flour, salt and soda, and add the creamed mixture.
Blend well and stir in oats
Drop by teaspoons onto greased cookie sheets
Bake at 350 degrees between 12 - 15 minutes
**For variety, you can add chopped nuts, raisins, chocolate chips or coconut. Makes about 5 dozen cookies.*

LEMONADE

4 cups of sugar
4 cups of fresh lemon juice
2-3 sliced lemons
In a sauce pan heat the sugar in 4 cups of water until sugar is dissolved and the mixture is hot
Allow to cool completely
Place in large serving container
Add 2 gallons of cold water, the lemon juice and lemon slices
Chill and stir
Pour over ice in glasses.

CHAPTER 26
AFTER THE SUMMER

POTATO-LEEK SOUP

8 cups of chicken broth
2 tablespoons (1/4 cup) of butter
6 medium potatoes, peeled and diced
1 cup of sour cream
6 celery stalks, cut and diced
Chopped fresh chives to garnish
3 medium leeks (including 2/3 of green part) trimmed, well washed and diced
Combine broth with salt and pepper to taste
Put in 3 to 4 quart saucepan over medium–high heat
Add potatoes, celery, and leeks.
Reduce heat to medium, cover and cook until the vegetables are tender (about 20 minutes)
Puree vegetables in batches with some liquid in a blender or processor
Return puree to saucepan, blending well. Place over medium heat
Add butter, stirring until melted
**Ladle into bowls, top with sour cream and chives and serve*

CARROT CAKE

2 cups of sugar
1 teaspoon of soda
2 cups of flour
2 teaspoons of cinnamon
1 teaspoon of baking powder
1/2 teaspoon of salt
Add 1 1/4 cup of cooking oil, 4 eggs and 3 cups of grated raw carrots
Mix well and add 1 1/2 cup chopped nuts
Bake 50 minutes in 350 degree oven. When done, take from oven
When warm, ice with the following:
1 package of powdered sugar
1 cube of butter
1 8 ounce package of cream cheese
2 teaspoons vanilla
Mix all together and ice warm cake

BEST BISCUITS

2 cups sifted flour
4 teaspoons baking powder
½ teaspoon salt
2/3 cup of milk
2 tablespoons sugar
½ cup shortening
1 egg unbeaten
½ teaspoon cream of tartar

Sift flour, salt, sugar, baking powder and cream of tartar into a bowl.
Add shortening and mix until a cornmeal-like consistency
Pour milk into batch and slowly add the egg.
Stir until a stiff dough
Knead 4 times and pat ½ inch thick
Cut with a biscuit cutter and bake 10-15 minutes at 450 degrees

GRAVY

Fry some bacon or ham in a skillet. Remove bacon or ham and keep the drippings
Add flour a little at a time to the skillet, stirring constantly to make a paste
Add milk a little at a time, stirring to remove any lumps
Add flour and milk as needed to make as much as you need
Add salt and pepper to taste
Serve on the biscuits with bacon or ham.

About the Author

Terry Wolfe grew up on a working cattle ranch on the west side of Colorado Springs, Colorado where wild animals would mix with the changing of the season and life had a sense of awe and wonder.

Made in the USA
Charleston, SC
10 November 2015